# PRAISE FOR

# Spider Tapestries

"Readers, be warned: Mike Allen will infect your subconscious with hallucinatory and alarming delight. This book is a must-read for fans of weird fiction and dark fantasy."
—Helen Marshall, World Fantasy Award-winning author of *Hair Side, Flesh Side* and *Gifts for the One Who Comes After*

"There was a time before the marketplace sliced our wild fantastic literature into bite sized chunks, a time when visions could be astounding, amazing, and weird all at once, a time when Clark Ashton Smith could mainline a Thousand and One Nights into million-colored suns. Now comes Mike Allen, shredding raw that scar-woven shroud between then, now, and infinity, releasing hallucinatory torrents of jewel-encrusted erotic transhumanism with the intensity of a quasar and stripping bare the secret wheels and cogs of the universe beside those lovers who would destroy them. Here are stories accelerating divine sibling rivalries into ultimate cosmic horror and offering unthinkable sacrifices to mark mere step stones on journeys redefining time, space, and identity ... dangerous short stories, not padded doorstops, epic explosions out of almost microscopic doses. More than a simple collection, these seven tales overlap and interplay in a crystalline cubist web that might as easily be the nightmares of deities or the dead dreams of a painted cranium, pirated memories or the visions gifted in an azure star spider's bite. Surrender yourself to *The Spider Tapestries* and let these tales rewire your mind past genre for a while—a while woven out of an eternity."
—Scott Nicolay, World Fantasy Award-winning author of *Do You Like to Look at Monsters?* and *Ana Kai Tangata*

"Elegant language and surrealistic themes defy genre and moral expectations in the weird and transgressive stories found in this collection . . . Echoes of Dunsany's myth making crash against nihilistic visionaries struggling for self and sanity, and often the only salvation is escaping into the imagination . . . Allen's pairing of individualistic suffering and cosmic hugeness evokes a lyrical friction between dread and wonder."

—*Publishers Weekly*

"The aptly named *Spider Tapestries* forms a stunning picture that is equal parts darkness and light . . . a whirlwind tour through worlds of decadent fantasy, noir-touched future-weird, and elegant horror. Mike Allen offers up intricate mythologies that feel real and lived in, rich-detailed stories for readers to immerse themselves in, and from which they will emerge changed. The stories feel epic in scope, from an assassin climbing through the clockwork gears of the world to rescue a goddess in a cage, to an AI moving through bodies and networks to gather up and reassemble the pieces of his lost love. Allen takes readers on a journey through years and worlds, all in the space of a few pages."

—A.C. Wise, author of *The Ultra Fabulous Glitter Squadron Saves the World Again*

"We think of science fiction, fantasy, and horror as genres of the imagination, but someone like Mike Allen shows us how lacking in daring and vision so many of their works can be, by resisting the labels altogether. *The Spider Tapestries* is kaleidoscopically, gloriously imaginative—feverish and fantastical—while never threatening to spin away into the nonsensical. Beyond the gorgeous and poetic mind pictures, he creates real, powerful emotions in the most alien of settings and circumstances. Allen achieves what I find most exciting in any artistic medium: a synthesis of beauty and the grotesque."

—Jeffrey Thomas, author of *Punktown*

"*The Spider Tapestries* by Mike Allen . . . smashes genre boundaries with a wrecking ball."

—Nicole Kornher-Stace, author of *Archivist Wasp*

# The Spider Tapestries

# Also by Mike Allen

*Novels*

THE BLACK FIRE CONCERTO
THE GHOULMAKER'S ARIA (forthcoming)

*Story Collections*

UNSEAMING
THE SKY-RIDERS (with Paul Dellinger)

*Poetry Collections*

HUNGRY CONSTELLATIONS
THE JOURNEY TO KAILASH
STRANGE WISDOMS OF THE DEAD
DISTURBING MUSES
PETTING THE TIME SHARK
DEFACING THE MOON

*As Editor*

CLOCKWORK PHOENIX 5

MYTHIC DELIRIUM: VOLUME TWO (with Anita Allen)

MYTHIC DELIRIUM (with Anita Allen)

CLOCKWORK PHOENIX 4

CLOCKWORK PHOENIX 3: New Tales of Beauty and Strangeness

CLOCKWORK PHOENIX 2: More Tales of Beauty and Strangeness

CLOCKWORK PHOENIX: Tales of Beauty and Strangeness

MYTHIC 2

MYTHIC

THE ALCHEMY OF STARS:
Rhysling Award Winners Showcase (with Roger Dutcher)

NEW DOMINIONS: Fantasy Stories by Virginia Writers

# MIKE ALLEN

## seven strange stories

Introduction by Nicole Kornher-Stace

**Charles County Public Library**
www.ccplonline.org

**Mythic Delirium**
**B O O K S**

mythicdelirium.com

# The Spider Tapestries

Copyright © 2016 by Mike Allen

Front cover photo by Ben Heys. Back cover photo by reddz. Licensed by 123RF.

Cover design © 2015 by Mike Allen

ISBN-10: 0988912465
ISBN-13: 978-0-9889124-6-5

FIRST EDITION
March 1, 2016

Published by Mythic Delirium Books
http://mythicdelirium.com

"Introduction" copyright © 2016 by Nicole Kornher-Stace.
"The Spider Tapestries" first appeared in *Lackington's* 8, Fall 2015.
"Sleepless, Burning Life" first appeared in *Steam-Powered: Lesbian Steampunk Stories*, ed. JoSelle Vanderhooft, Torquere Books, 2011.
"Twa Sisters" first appeared in *Not One of Us* 47, 2012.
"Silent in Her Nest" is original to this collection.
"She Who Runs" first appeared in *Sky Whales and Other Wonders*, ed. Vera Nazarian, Norilana Books, 2009.
"Stolen Souls" first appeared in *Altair* 3, 1999.
"Still Life with Skull" first appeared in *Solaris Rising 2: The New Solaris Book of Science Fiction*, ed. Ian Whates, Solaris, 2013.

Our gratitude goes out to the following who because of their generosity are from now on designated as supporters of Mythic Delirium Books: Saira Ali, Cora Anderson, Anonymous, Patricia M. Cryan, Steve Dempsey, Oz Drummond, Patrick Dugan, Matthew Farrer, C. R. Fowler, Mary J. Lewis, Paul T. Muse, Jr., Shyam Nunley, Finny Pendragon, Kenneth Schneyer, and Delia Sherman.

*For Ian Watson*

# ACKNOWLEDGMENTS

As with my previous collection, *Unseaming*, the stories in this book span a period of sixteen years, so I must apologize up front if I fail to give credit where it is due. My gratitude goes out to the following who had a hand in bringing these stories into being: R.H.W. Dillard, Jeanne Larsen, Catherine Reniere, Robert N. Stephenson, Vera Nazarian, JoSelle Vanderhooft, John Benson, Ian Whates, Ranylt Richildis, Ian Watson, Alexandra Seidel, Virginia M. Mohlere, Sally Brackett Robertson, Ed Allen, Francesca Forrest, Shveta Thakrar, Elizabeth Campbell, Christina Sng, Nicole Kornher-Stace, Domink Parisien, Sonya Taaffe, Laird Barron, Patty Templeton, Amal El-Mohtar, Julia Rios, C.S.E. Cooney, Alessandro Bavari and everyone who backed the *Clockwork Phoenix 5* Kickstarter. And, of course, Anita Allen above all.

I want to single out Sonya Taaffe for her invaluable help with ancient names and languages; Cathy Reniere, for showing me how to bring the demons to the surface of "Stolen Souls"; Patty Templeton for introducing me to the art of Alessandro Bavari, which, combined with a challenge from Nicole Kornher-Stace to compose a story the way I compose poems, led directly to the writing of "Twa Sisters." Thanks, too, to Nicole for her kind introductory words, which led me to work harder for this book than I might have otherwise.

I have just a few words to share about the stories themselves. The beginning of "Stolen Souls" was the final piece I wrote in pursuit of my master's degree in creating writing from Hollins College. Five years later the story became my first to be purchased by a professional market. As such, I will always see it as the first major crossing of my career. "Still Life With Skull" is a direct sequel to "Twa Sisters," though it may not be readily apparent. Finally, "Silent in Her Nest" is both a companion piece and counterargument to my story "Her Acres of Pastoral Playground" that appeared in *Unseaming*, something I doubt anyone would catch on to if I didn't just baldly state it.

—Mike Allen, Roanoke, Va., November 2015

# TABLE OF CONTENTS

# INTRODUCTION
## Nicole Kornher-Stace

Like many, I first became aware of Mike Allen's work as a celebrated poet and editor. (Specifically because in his capacity *as* an editor he rejected one of *my* poems, but that's neither here nor there.) Reading his poetry I was immediately impressed by the depth and the voice and the *scope* of the stuff, blurring back and forth across boundaries of form and tone and genre at top speed and with immense surety. Fluidity of voice like that is a powerful tool to keep the reader on her toes, disrupting expectations in the best possible way. Read enough of it—or, better yet, attend one of his readings and *listen*—and you start to suspect he's toying with you. If, that is, you're the kind of person who likes your reading material easy to shelve by genre.

Remember that; it'll be important in a minute.

While Mike Allen was piling up his Rhysling wins, publishing his speculative poetry/fiction zine *Mythic Delirium*, and putting together the critically-acclaimed *Clockwork Phoenix* weird fiction anthology series, he was also busily plugging away at amassing a significant body of his own short fiction, including the Nebula finalist "The Button Bin." Bizarrely, or maybe not, given his tremendous success in the poetry and editorial fields, for years Allen's reputation as a poet and editor eclipsed the one he was quietly developing as a writer of short fiction.

Until, that is, the release of his first short fiction collection, *Unseaming*, in 2014. With which, in the words of Laird Barron's introduction, Allen "immediately made a case for his inclusion at the forefront of the New New Wave" of a new golden age of horror. Within that genre, Allen still put on full display that remarkable flexibility of form and tone that he honed in his years as a poet: it's horror, but it also borrows from pretty much every corner of speculative fiction, and the end result is multilayered and complex. And yet, in the words of Thomas Ligotti's blurb of that book, "*fun*. Not 'good' fun, and certainly not 'good clean' fun. They are too unnerving for those modifiers, too serious, like laughter in the dark . . ."

Remember that too.

In his latest collection, *The Spider Tapestries*, Allen outdoes himself even further, borrowing and synthesizing across genres with gleeful abandon. Having made a name for himself as poet and editor, then proving with *Unseaming* that he can crank out top-shelf horror fiction with the best of them, the subsequent *The Spider Tapestries* feels like the throwing down of a gauntlet to anyone who so much as thinks of pigeonholing the versatile body of work of which Mike Allen is capable.

Here, then, we witness an adept blending of Allen's poetry and horror toolboxes. The muscular, vivid prose and genre mashuppery of the former; the disquieting ambience and characterization of the latter. This results in stories like "Twa Sisters," with an atmosphere and setting as if Heironymous Bosch had been brought in as a consultant on *Blade Runner*. Or "Sleepless, Burning Life," which, with simultaneous nods to steampunk and metaphysics, explores and upends the familiar trope of Mortal Chosen by the Gods. Or "Stolen Souls," a hard SFnal noir piece whose alien thugs are named after characters in ancient mythology.

Meanwhile *The Spider Tapestries* seems at times to be in conversation with *Unseaming*: the future-tech body modifications of the former echoing the present-day body horror of the latter; the monstrous visitations in *Unseaming* presaging the self-made monstrosities in *The Spider Tapestries*. If in *Unseaming*, monsters are Lovecraftian and unknowable, in *The Spider Tapestries* they've become part of the everyday landscape.

Under all of it, though, runs that aforementioned current of *fun*. There's a definite sense that while Allen is borrowing from these various themes and materials, he's poking at them as well. From lampooning the hard-boiled detective narrative voice ("From the waist down, she had me at hello, which she didn't say, because she had no mouth.") to parodying a Tarantino-esque over-the-top glorification of violence ("Velvet blood geysered into the air, and even its innards were achingly beautiful as they spilled wet and gelatinous into the void beyond the sprocket's tooth-studded edge.").

A further, deeper layer of his collections and anthologies alike involves the collaboration of his wife, artist Anita Allen. She arranges the stories in such a way that each book reads like a concept album, full of callbacks and refrains to earlier material, foreshadowing to the pieces that come later. *The Spider Tapestries*, with its tendency to hopscotch back and forth across genre lines, highlights her contribution to great effect. There is a sense, deliberately uncomfortable though not at all unpleasant, of being shuttled back and forth across those boundaries, from timeless mythos to slick future tech, so smoothly and deliberately that the word "tapestries" in the title hardly feels coincidental.

A fascinating incursion into and across any number of genres and themes, *The Spider Tapestries* adroitly continues the upward trajectory begun with *Unseaming* and guarantees Allen a place high on the writers-to-watch list of any reader who appreciates vividly original work that defies easy categorization.

In the meantime, though, enjoy.

# THE SPIDER TAPESTRIES

The azure star spider injects ink when it bites, an umber venom that paints the veins if the skin has paled enough, that steeps the brain in a fire of extrasensory comprehension. We collect its poison in the wild, on cautious days-long crawls through the caverns formed by the roots of the blood-scented basalt trees, whose crowns cannot be seen beneath the ever-present cloud cover.

Though the spider-mothers are quick and fearsome, their phosphorescent legs longer than our fingers, they present the least of the threats that wait. The beacon mantis opens the lamps of its many eyes to blind us, and sometimes the visors we wear fail to darken their tints in time, leave us paralyzed and blinking, primed to be dragged off in its long jaws.

On truly unfortunate journeys, the incisor gods that scavenge between the great fissures of bark fail to harvest enough mewling grubs to sate their hunger, and descend on all nine paws into the root tunnels, investigating the noises we make as we crawl. Our maps guide us along paths excavated deep and narrow to keep the holy teeth from finding purchase in our backs, but the gods are clever and ruled by their appetites, so our engineering is not always enough. It is rare for a harvest season to pass without a crawler giving up her life in an agonizing sacrifice that lets the rest of an expedition escape.

Charming the spider-mothers with plucks on the disordered lyres of their webs, delicately milking their fangs with soft metal thimbles, these things hardly seem frightening in comparison.

The crawlers who return to our hive are greeted with unblinking eyes and limbs lifted in silent, reverential dance. The leader of the foray will pass her first primed vial to the dancers, who will unstop it and paint their tongues umber. Their breath becomes heady ambrosia on the instant, and the exhausted crawlers will open their own mouths to receive kisses and then collapse. The terrors and wonders they experienced during their expedition will transfer to the dancers during the touch of tongues, and the dancers will retract their eyes as the visions fill their ganglia, guide their spines. They will dance blind, yet never stumble. Their feet will beat a history in the soft earth. They will weep, their voices rising to score the names of the deceased into the salt spikes that stab slow from the vaults of our roofs.

They will dance until the chamber of return can no longer contain them, emerge into the tunnels reciting new verse in every contortion of muscle, bone, and chitin, accompany themselves with notes made from the scraping together of serrated legs.

We will understand their song without having heard a word. Their melodies and percussions will thrum through the stones and fissures of our homes, wash across our skins and shells. They will stay in motion until the poison coma takes them, and they collapse in crescents of paralysis, dreaming themselves as spider-mothers patiently mending webs, patiently awaiting prey.

It is not for us to taste the venom unfiltered as the dancers do. We cannot survive its visionary fire, though we all long for the strength to contain it in our veins. The vials brought back from the crawl will be taken to hollows in our city's iciest deeps and nestled in walls of yielding mud to ferment. That loam will release acrid scents of centipede treacle as it parts to receive our treasures.

High above the nests where we dwell, oven-warm chambers mirror the icy spaces underneath our halls and streets. Through the roofs of these rooms pierce wooden stalactites: the heavy branches of the eidolon shrubs, bent to the ground by their own weight, burrowing through toxic slag surface, past tangles of roots, through softened bedrock and further still, breaching into our space. Miraculously, the buried tips of their branches bear fruit, soft berries tinted blue (so claims the lore) as the sky our kind once knew.

Ten children will ascend there, chosen by their high marks at learning and their skills at weaving fiber and shaping clay. Hefting pails made from the shells of the most soft-spoken of their elders, these children are the only ones permitted to gather the berries, not for hygiene's sake or from any mystical notion of purity, but because they have proven themselves of the right mindframe. Their touch will color the juice with earnest curiosity and devotion to the furthering of the soul. Thus not one tender fruit need be discarded, even if it bursts.

Other ingredients we collect are more mundane: lichens peeled from our home gardens; meaty grubs from our terrariums; lush roots and sharp-flavored spores from the mosses that cluster around our lamps. These offerings are brought to the natural obelisk that rises from the shallow pool in the center of our northernmost plaza, a place where wares are sold, histories are read, laws debated and revised.

As we clean and cook, the protégés of the dancers prepare to stomp the berries. They pull on stockings spun from the webs of previous feasts, stitched in iridescent patterns that trick the eyes. The pails are arranged in interlocking triangles, and the stompers execute a puzzle dance, hopping from one pail to another without colliding or even letting their feet touch the ground between. At the end, they peel the stockings and leave them soaking in the juice. A smell of sweet nectar teases as the gossamer dissolves to fuel our next harvest of dreams.

Fetched from storage, the venom is dripped into each pail and thus transmuted, its mind-expanding effects strengthened through chemical bonding while its toxicity dilutes. The resulting jelly seasons the loaves of our celebratory meal.

Once we are fed, we settle in our slings to receive the gift of the spider-mothers, the warp and weft of a great new imagining, a blessing that lets us continue our lives of confinement without souring into rancor. Though we will dream but a few hours, we will spend a precious eternity inside the vistas of our minds acting as weavers of atoms and fate. We become like the spider-mothers, but we do not lie in wait to eat the weak and blind. We create tapestry in communion.

Emerging in our dreams from the shells where we have incubated, we project threads of our own, gentle nets to trap protean hallucinations, bind them into crystal-bright continents. Our perpendicular strands form latitude and longitude lines, link private myths into a map of our collective mirage, grant it weight, depth, texture. A new land so forged, we shall set off to explore.

Centuries will pass, so it will seem, before the dream fades. In that time we will toil and play under our long-lost suns. We will tend vast manses, not cut from the forests, but grown and shaped, generations raised in nature's embrace. In time, visitors cast in unfamiliar and beautiful shapes will arrive from outside our sky, and we will share our harvests with them, and eagerly learn everything they bring to teach us.

# SLEEPLESS, BURNING LIFE

*Climbing in the gears*
*above the Cosmic Sphere,*
*she pulls the pin*
*that spins the stars in place,*
*falls laughing*
*through the death of Forever.*

### One: The Search

Jyshiu awoke as the great gear began to turn beneath her, and sprang immediately to her feet, throwing her arms out to steady herself as her perch tilted.

She had taken stock of the immense clockwork before choosing her resting place, and knew she was in no imminent danger of being crushed, not for the first few moments of motion. As the teeth of the gear rose, they would lift her past another gear that spun flat on a vertical axis, she had already planned the leap to safety.

This was what Jyshiu's afterlife had been for countless years, perhaps even longer. She did not, in fact, know how long it had been since she left the body of her first flesh behind in the witches' cavern under the desert. She might have squeezed the poison from the spider's fangs onto her tongue only moments ago. Or her death might have taken place centuries ago—in which case not even her bones remained—as in exchange for the passage she had chosen, she had granted the witches permission to feast on her body if her heart had not begun to beat again when the sun next rose.

The witches, with their translucent skin shriveled to their bones and their eyes milky-white as semen, had not wished her well in her quest, not at all, but their appetites were such that they could never refuse so generous an offer. She had come to them with a body dense with strong muscle, sure to yield a harvest of healthy meat when their knives sliced deep through her weathered brown skin.

They had honored their word, and she cared not what they did with what remained of her.

She bent to spring as the gear she rode neared the crest of its rotation and the full expanse of the flat and saw blade-like gear that was her next place of purchase came into full view, turning faster than when she first observed it from below. She crouched further, leapt, and rolled with her arms pulled to her sides. A bruising impact on her left arm, another layer of blue contusion to add to the many, many already there.

But she looked up, and all the instincts of her heart and gut were proven blissfully true. As tears moistened and reddened her eyes, this pain endured by her body in the megacosm outside time all but disappeared from her notice.

Around her, above her, and most certainly beneath her, a dizzying array of mechanical components jerked and ground and whirled and rolled: pinions and spurs, beveled gears and crowns, sprockets and grooved spheres, harmonic drives infinitely nestled inside one another, turning in opposite directions, towers of interlocked stars ending in independent gears twirling in epicycles, some gears themselves as large as continents interlocking with others further distant, big as planets, worm screws so far distant they might appear as galaxies if seen spinning on end. Some configurations of racks and rings and helixes were so complex they formed recognizable shapes: birds or prowling cats or whales, titanic things that moved within the machinery on tracks and patterns that only the mad maker of the cosmic clockwork could understand.

In the epoch outside time's flow that Jyshiu had spent climbing her maddening, methodical way through the cosmic gears, these marvels had become a common sight. The thing that blew joy into her heart dangled far above all these, gyrating wildly at the apex of the dome that could only be the curve of the celestial ceiling, blazing with uncountable lights in colors the eyes of her abandoned physical body could never have perceived.

The object that hung above all the gears in the great mechanism was a cage. The eternal prison of Amritu the Sleepless. In all this endless ascent, Jyshiu had never once actually laid eyes on her cage.

It was this she intended to reach. Because the goddess trapped inside had once begged her for help. Begged her to finally bring her sleep. Inside that cage, Amritu danced, and thrashed, and writhed, and ran, and beat her fists on the floor, stood up and cartwheeled in never ending motion, and no matter how much she exerted, no matter how exhausted she became, stillness was denied her. Her body in its torment beat asymmetrical rhythms on the drum of the cage floor, and those vibrations, the paroxysms of a goddess, carried up through the layered wires of the cage mesh, becoming currents of power. The Sleepless One served as a living battery, the dark-eyed dancer who made the cosmos turn.

If she ever slept, all the workings of the universe would freeze and fall apart. And this was what Jyshiu wanted, more than the continuation of her own life.

She had left her body behind and climbed forever in the cosmic clockwork to bring Amritu the one thing she could never have: peace.

She adjusted the pair of knives sheathed on either side of the belt circling her waist. She had purchased them with her own blood from the Seer at Amarah: strange weapons with oddly wide and thick blades. The Seer's lips had been death-cold as she drank at the wound in Jyshiu's wrist, but the price had been worth it. She'd spoken truth, that the knives would follow her into the afterlife, would obey her command and hers alone, would cut even the divine. The prophetess had told her where to find the witches who would send her on, and what sort of world awaited her.

Jyshiu understood that it was not the cage above her that pivoted and orbited so wildly. She stood on a moving platform inside a vast mechanical orrery that was itself in motion, and contained within it a large contraption that also moved. The cage was fixed in place, the only constant in this infinite machine. The fact that she could now see it meant that at least she could measure her journey and its conclusion in terms that resembled the finite.

How appropriate that in the impoverished origins of the strange life she had left behind, a tiny act of rebellion had yielded a blossom the size of a sun gone nova, had led her down the path to the ultimate rebellion, the one that would be the Final Act in the story of everything.

Her first memories involved looking out at the ocean of the coastal city of Yrelhys through the narrow eyehole of her hood. It wasn't until she was older, old enough to hold a broom and sweep at her mother's request or sit on the floor to dine with the adults instead of at the small pantry table, that she began to wonder why no girl she knew was made to dress in public as she did, with a white covering from head to ankle. Her pious parents refused to speak of it, and her father threatened beatings when she even dared to ask, though he clearly had not the heart to follow through.

Finally, her mother, after a secret late night indulgence in wine, told her it was because of the birthmark on the her shoulder: a bizarre spiraling sunburst with zigzag arms. And it was because of this birthmark that the other strange restriction on Jyshiu's life existed. When her family went to worship at the temple of Amritu the Sleepless, she was confined to the chapel for the unclean above the narthex, with its eerie honeycomb of holes in the walls that carried the sounds of worship in from the nave proper. She was not allowed to come into the space where the priestess of Amritu danced and thrashed in her cage.

Her mother told her that she and her father did not know why, only that the priest of Kitsartu, the supreme goddess who oversaw all births and all deaths, had told them this must be so or death would come to their daughter before her thread could untwine itself from the three interlocked wheels of mortal life. Once Jyshiu knew this her life became a cauldron of anguish and resentment. The songs she heard through the temple pipes were so beautiful in their sadness that she longed to stand before the cage in the chancel and hear that warbling throat full on.

When she was sixteen she took a knife and cut the flesh from her shoulder. Every scrap of it. For a time her mother's wails echoed in her head, even more hauntingly than those of the unseen priestess. Yet, when the circle of raw flesh scarred over, the mark returned.

The next year her mother arranged her marriage. When word came that the zeppelin carrying her husband-to-be and his entourage had left the port of Teass in the far north, her heart began to pound in a way she'd never experienced before—a frightening way, a despairing way. Her parents and her siblings told her it was because of her husband's approach and the bliss of her impending wedding. None gave any thought to the revelation she'd been given by Kitsartu's priests that once she was pendulous with child she would be barred for good from the grounds of the Sleepless One's basilica. And again, there was no explanation; it was Kitsartu's will.

None in the temple had ever seen her uncovered. When she stepped demurely through the arch, clad in a thin and sea-blue dress she had only been permitted to wear in the sand-colored halls of her family's home, the guards in the alcoves took no notice. Her waves of earth-brown hair were wound in a respectful trio of wheel-like buns, and the Sleepless One's sigil, the Weeping Eye, adorned her tawny brow in proper blue and black. The only oddity in her clothing was a shawl that covered her shoulders. But this was the morning service, not the evening worship her parents attended daily, and the bustling, brightly-clothed crowd kept her anonymous as she let herself be carried through the nave on the human current, her heart speeding even faster than their feet. Surely her household had already noticed she was missing, and if the priest's words at her birth were to be believed, what she was about to see would kill her.

She didn't care. Her heart continued to race as she beheld the vaulted ceiling and its mosaics of mechanical beasts and beings:

the lamps with their green and blue flames that made walking on
the tilted floor feel like descending through the sea; the lamps the
color of blood-gorged flesh that bathed the great metal object hung
above the altar, the cage that held a woman clad in a loose robe woven from her own black hair. She knelt with her head bowed, her
face hidden beneath her hair.

In a semicircle below her the acolyte priestesses knelt, their
nakedness concealed only by the varying length of their hair, and
the tall drums held between their knees.

When the great doors to nave shut, the acolytes began to
drum. A male voice from behind a screen led a prayer, speaking
in rhythm to the drumbeat, and the gathered worshipers chanted,
mourning their goddess's suffering even as they wished her eternal
wakefulness. They picked up the basic rhythm and continued it as
the acolytes began to build upon it in more and more complicated
layers. Meanwhile, the priestess in the cage started her dance, a
seemingly random flow of mounting sinuous frenzy. It continued
until she was throwing herself against the bars with no apparent
concern for the effect of the impacts on her dusky skin. Her dance
grew even more terrifying to behold, but Jyshiu saw no blood. And
then the priestess began to sing, and Jyshiu thought her rib cage
would break. The notes carried an unearthly purity, and she wept
that for all of her life she had only heard such a wonder muffled
through a wall.

And yet . . . the throng she stood among was also moved to
tears, to howls, to blubbering. She could recall no such noise heard
through the pipes, but she did not ponder the matter long, nor did
she give more than a fleeting thought to the abrupt, searing pain
in her scarred shoulder. In fact, it wasn't until she laid her palms
on the cold of the bars that she comprehended that she had walked
all the way up to the altar and wrapped her fingers around the
metal poles at a level even with the priestess' knees. The woman's
legs were slender and muscular as a horse's flank. She had stopped
dancing, though she tipped her head back and sang with a volume that should have shredded her vocal chords down to a croak.
No one had stopped Jyshiu; Everyone, even the acolytes, now lay
glassy-eyed on the floor.

The priestess fell to all fours before Jyshiu, still singing. And then she stopped, and opened her eyes. They were black like dried blood and yet depthless. Tears like ink ran from their corners.

Jyshiu's shoulder burned with the heat of a crematorium.

"Help me," the priestess said, in a voice even stranger and more stunning than her song—as if a mouth had opened in a stormy ocean. "Help me," she said, and seized Jyshiu's arm, the one marred with scar and birthmark. And Jyshiu felt wet kisses on her wrist, felt a nip of teeth. "Help me," the voice begged again. A sensation like electricity blazed over every inch of Jyshiu's skin as the priestess pressed herself against the bars, pressed Jyshiu's wrist between the softness of her breasts, pressed her palm flat so she could feel the other woman's heart hammering impossibly fast and hard, like a piston driven by overheated steam. Then the priestess pulled Jyshiu's hand up to her lips, brushed them against the tips of her fingers. "Help me," she said again in that impossible voice.

She took the index and middle fingers in her mouth, and slid her lips down to the bottom knuckles. Suckled. Jyshiu felt her tongue. And the sensation of electricity coursed through her to the point of pain, throbbing in her temples, her neck, the backs of her eyes, between her thighs, curling in her nipples, piercing the soles of her feet. Here was the death foretold, a death she desired with all her being.

She wailed, and broke from the priestess' grip.

If she had thought the voice of the woman in the cage sounded inhuman before, that impression was eclipsed by the howl that ruptured from the priestess' impossibly distended mouth.

Stones fell into the nave, striking amidst the dazed and newly conscious worshipers, as the temple ceiling split.

Jyshiu survived not just the chaos but the capture and lashing that followed, and the tumble down unforgiving rock into the oubliette. When she awoke in a bizarre and impossibly large cage flooded with light, it took her several confused moments before she deduced she was actually dreaming.

The dream surely had to be her brain's bewildered deconstruction of the madness she'd just been party to, for across the great multi-stellated polygon that formed the floor—a curving silver column of cage bar rising from the tip of each of the points at its bewildering edge—the priestess danced, with a manic energy that made the display in the temple seem little more than a child skipping. When she twirled, her dark cascade of ankle-length hair, no longer bound to her body, would rise like a spun skirt. Jyshiu could see how the woman's constant unearthly movements coursed up the length of her slender nut-brown body: from ankle to knee to bare hips and buttocks, belly and spine, breasts and shoulders, neck and narrow chin, sinewed arms, tapering wrists and long, graceful fingers that flexed with the hypnotic grace of running water.

The sight crushed her heart in a fist and stole the air from her lungs.

Then the dancer flung herself at the floor, and the derangement of the movement was terrifying. Even at this distance, Jyshiu felt the thunder of the impact through her own feet. Her hair splaying beneath her in a haphazard mattress, the woman jerked and spasmed on her back in a joint-wrenching fit, every strike against the floor vibrating with the tremor of a titanic drum. She cried out, and Jyshiu's legs lurched her forward almost of their own accord. She wanted to help. Yet she was frightened for them both and those emotions were nearly overwhelmed by the woman's unbearable beauty. The dancer moaned, an utterance that somehow fused deep despair and transcendent fervor, and arched her entire body from heels to shoulders, thrusting her hips into the air as she rolled her head back and forth in a pose that aped both agony and orgasm, and Jyshiu stumbled to all fours. A hunger opened in her, a pit of desire that completely unlocked her, an urge to fill any emptiness with this woman in front of her. The urge was so overpowering it paralyzed Jyshiu.

A splash of darkness made Jyshiu look down. There was blood on the floor below her face. She touched her fingers to the moistness on her cheek that she had subconsciously taken for tears, and pulled them back to discover she was weeping blood.

She raised her eyes to discover the dancer staring at her, still locked in that impossibly beautiful arch with every muscle trembling, her arms twisting with painful grace, unable to stop moving.

The dancer's eyes were black with blood that fanned across her face in all directions. She worked her lips, repeating a syllable that slowly became louder. "Why . . . why . . . why . . . "

Jyshiu spoke a name that her mind had refused to form. "Amritu."

The goddess stretched an arm toward her. "Why did you run from me . . . why . . . why . . . help . . . help . . . help me . . . "

The gesture tore through her even as longing twisted her insides. She made herself crawl forward and then pushed to her feet, but could not make herself run. Amritu continued to reach for her, spasms rolling up her spine, the motion leaving Jyshiu dizzy. The goddess continued to mouth a silent plea for help that Jyshiu finally answered when she was close enough that a leap would put her in the being's grasp. "I don't know what you want me to do."

"Bring me peace, love," the goddess said. "Make me still." And when Amritu spoke the word "love," the pit of longing in Jyshiu became an abyss, though she didn't understand why.

Amritu cried out and flipped onto her belly, thrashed toward Jyshiu, the concussion of her movement shaking the entire cage. It took all Jyshiu's strength to keep her balance, but she involuntarily took a step away. The goddess' wail was hardly louder than a whisper: "No. No. Don't run from me." Shame heated Jyshiu's chest even as her fear made her knees tremble. The goddess lay prone at her feet, hair covering her back and thighs in a translucent veil. The scent of her, a musk of earth and nectar and smoke, fogging Jyshiu's head.

The goddess raised a hand again, reached, and Jyshiu abruptly became conscious of her own nakedness. She was not, despite what she insisted to her mother, a virgin, and the two boys and one girl who had secretly beheld her so in her two decades of life had found her pleasing, but she saw her body as an awkward stack of bulges and sags, nothing that held the grace of athleticism or art; compared to the vision at her feet she was a mere lump of wax. And yet another part of her clamorous mind wondered that she could be so overwhelmed at this moment by certainty of her unworthiness: Amritu still extended her arm, visibly struggling to keep the gesture gentle, until her hand hovered just an inch above Jyshia's foot. The goddess raised on her other elbow, and it was then that Jyshiu saw the spiraling zigzag starbust on Amritu's shoulder . . . on her left shoulder, an opposite to the scar on Jyshiu's right. What did it mean? She did not know.

The goddess curled her fingers around Jyshiu's ankle. Her pale palm pressed against Jyshiu's skin, and if the sight of Amritu's nakedness had seemed impossible to bear Jyshiu learned in that instant that it was nothing compared to the goddess' touch. A current bolted through her body, triggered every nerve ending. But before she could even cry out Amritu had pulled herself forward, pressed her moist lips to the inside of Jyshiu's ankle, and that current redoubled a thousand fold. The ache of longing that hummed through the core of Jyshiu's body surged and peaked, and her mind ignited white.

When her vision returned she lay on her back, that skin-burning current pulsing through her in waves. Her disoriented brain told her something that couldn't be possible, and when she raised her head the sight proved more impossible yet—the goddess met her gaze, her dark and exquisite chin just a knuckle's width above Jyshiu's navel. She twitched, and Jyshiu's felt the goddess' ribs and flanks shift against her thighs.

"You'll kill me," she told Amritu, her entire body a coliseum of racing blood and electricity.

"I have to," the goddess breathed, "I have to . . . make sure . . . make sure." She rocked back, kissed her mortal lover in the indentation of her right hip. The goddess' kiss set off a nova in her flesh.

Her vision returned, and Amritu's eyes stared right into her own. Jyshiu couldn't help but whimper when her hitching ribs would even let her breathe. The Sleepless One lay beside her, one thigh over her belly, the full length of her body pressed against Jyshiu's shivering flesh. "I can't let you forget," the goddess said. Then she seized her head and silenced Jyshiu's gasp with her own mouth, her hair sheeting over both of them like a warm cocoon.

That Jyshiu's soul continued to exist, that her brain continued to perceive, seemed a miracle to her. The taste of Amritu's breath, of her skin, of her tongue, crumpled Jyshiu's mind like so much paper. The anima of the goddess blazed through her from scalp to toe tip, and she spontaneously came against her divine lover. Amritu hummed, savoring the kiss—Jyshiu struggled to breathe but didn't have the strength to break away, didn't want to try. She came again even before she noticed the goddess' fingers flowing over her, dancing up and down her body. She bucked, practically screaming down the goddess' throat, a noise Amritu eagerly swallowed as those sure and supple fingers found the folds between Jyshiu's legs, slid into her with ease. And they danced, against and inside her, even the first touch enough to bring her to joint-wrenching, muscle-tearing orgasm, but Amritu didn't let go, and she died under the goddess' urgent strokes, again and again and again.

She didn't know when the kiss at last broke off, because Amritu's fingers still moved inside her, but at some point she realized she could see the vast cosmic arch of the cage, that the goddess' face with its streaks of blood radiating from her eyes no longer eclipsed her vision. She heard that voice supple as ocean say, "Now, love, you can find me." Then the goddess kissed her right breast, tongued her nipple, took it in her mouth. Jyshiu howled as she burned into oblivion—

—and woke again in darkness, nerves still jangling from a dream that had been more vivid than anything she'd experienced, even when awake. At first, lying on the cold stone, she railed at her own arrogance, that her mind could allow such a thing even in dream. In the black of the oubliette, she oscillated between a longing so deep she thought she would die from it and a frantic certainty that everything she felt had been delusion.

That doubt vanished when the acolytes came for her, and the priestess of the temple fainted when the guards drew Jyshiu out into the torchlight.

Amritu had branded her in a way that could never be mistaken. In every place she'd been touched by the goddess' lips—her right ankle, her right hip, her right breast, her mouth—a new zig-zag starburst spiraled out, stark white against the dark olive of her skin. The jagged arms of the spiral radiated from her lips to cover her face, her scalp, her ears, her neck, her collarbone, where they overlapped with the arms of the starburst centered on her now-pearl-white nipple. She was harmed no more but cast from the temple by servants whose eyes were round with fright, tossed into the next leg of her life's journey.

Even as Jyshiu stood upon the great gear here in the regions outside time, the spirals bestowed by the goddess' lips marked her leg, her chest, her face.

The marks on her body didn't yet burn with the white-hot fever of the goddess' awareness, but soon, soon they would sear so sweet.

Her vantage point turned, and Jyshiu beheld an object far above her that had not been present a moment before when she had stared up at the cage: a great face, white as a full moon with wide-set eyes darker than the death of all suns. Pitiless and frozen, vast black-lipped mouth a cold line, the face of the goddess Kitsartu projected above the cosmic clockwork she designed and peered into depths that only her mind could comprehend in full. The flow in Jyshiu's veins froze in response—had the Mother of Life and Death, the murderous genius who built the universe, spied the mite loose in her machine?

Jyshiu went sprawling as the gear she stood upon stopped spinning.

She recovered immediately, to see that all the grinding and whirling about her had shuddered to a halt. And in that sudden silence, a new noise, a rhythmic patter, increased in volume with alarming speed. Someone naïve to the region outside all times might have mistaken the noise for drumming, but Jyshiu knew exactly what it was: running footsteps, the bare feet of headless giants unleashed by Kitsartu to hunt the contamination in their midst.

She sprinted pell-mell, leapt onto a vertically mounted gear no wider than a writing tablet, and hurtled up its teeth two at a time as if they were stairs. She gripped the pommels of her knives and drew them, one clutched in each fist as she bounded to the crest of the gear and flung herself off at the next one, a titled sprocket with its teeth cast at a dangerous, sloping bevel.

She didn't turn her head, but at the angle she now scrambled, her pursuers couldn't be missed.

Like predatory statues come to life, towers of golden skin and sharp-etched muscle, two Headless Ones loped toward her, their chests and arms like moving granite, veined penises flopping above thighs thick as tree trunks, the junctures where their necks had once risen from their shoulders now scooped out hollows stretched over with that same skin of perfect gold. With no sense accessible but touch, they still homed in on her, detecting her presence through sheer divinity.

In the seaside city, before her act of temple-destroying rebellion, she had sat veiled behind a screen in the back of class and heard the conflicting stories of the Headless Ones, the host of lesser deities who performed all the physical tasks that kept the cosmos running. Once they had heads gorgeous as their bodies, but Kitsartu convinced them that their bodily urges and desires created a distraction that had to be disposed of to keep all the myriad worlds and their peoples in proper obeisance. So adamant was the goddess in her logic that these beings willingly gave up their heads, which were gathered by Kitsartu in a tower of jars connected by bone conduits to allow them all to link mind to mind. And here the theologians' claims divided: Some asserted that Kitsartu's attempt to build a supermind had failed, that the gods in their jars remained just as obsessed with gossip and grudges and gross lusts and grosser schemes as they had before they gave their bodies up, and in a rage the Mother of Death disconnected them from the cosmos; Others held that Kitsartu had never intended to let them meld their minds with the universe or each other, and she had locked them away once the trick was sprung, keeping their bodies as servants to clean and to repair.

And to hunt intruders.

The pair gained on her with long, beast-quick strides, one of them already bounding up the thin vertical gear even as she balanced precariously at the point where the beveled sprocket wedged into a complex rack of thread-thin horizontal bars. Were the works to start moving again at that moment, she would immediately be pressed into the rack and shredded.

Jyshiu clambered on the rack, treating it like a ladder, though it offered her no more than shallow toeholds for her ascent.

Behind her the closest Headless One leaped onto the sprocket and kept coming.

She spoke the Word she had been given by the Seer at Amarah before she trekked into the desert. Then she flicked her wrists as if she cracked a pair of whips. The nestled blades-within-blades inside her short, thick knives came free, telescoped into vorpal-sharp swords longer than her arms. She dropped as the Headless One sprang to meet her, and plunged both blades into the indentation that once housed the god's neck. It reared back as she loosed a defiant scream and straddled the giant's meaty shoulder. Then she levered the swords as if she pushed shear handles apart. One blade sliced forward through collarbone, ribs and breastplate, the other through shoulder blade and spine.

The Headless One split like an opening scallop. Velvet blood geysered into the air, and even its innards were achingly beautiful as they spilled wet and gelatinous into the void beyond the sprocket's tooth-studded edge. Jyshiu half-fell, half-somersaulted from the divinity's split torso as its companion came at her, arms outstretched to grab her and pull her in half.

Luck and momentum threw her right between its arms. It pulled them closed to crush her, but she slipped through, slick with blood, and as she fell she slashed the blades in each hand out to either side before walloping her own head on the gear's beveled metal surface.

The second Headless One continued forward, both legs severed completely through shin and calf, and toppled over the edge after its companion.

Jyshiu groped for consciousness. She had landed in a groove between teeth and wedged the tips of her swords to either side like pitons. Their tips were so sharp they had actually gouged the metal, and it was this and her own struggle to hang onto awareness—and thus her grip—that kept her from tumbling off. After minutes of white-knuckle fighting, she won the struggle, and slowly managed to regain her feet.

Drenched head-to-toe in ichor from the hearts of gods, she peered up at the roof of the universe, where her goal was once again invisible, and knew it would not be long before she stood there in the flesh, reunited once more with her love, Kitsartu's prisoner.

The thought was like a roar of defiance, and though she made no noise, somewhere deep below, she felt a tremble in the cosmic machine.

## Two: The Truth

Her wish came true, though how long it took she could never have said: epochs, or perhaps mere minutes. Nonetheless, she never let her impatience betray her. She used the bound-together strips of her sliced-up tunic for a climbing belt, her retracted knives for pitons, and gripped with her toes where she could as she descended the chain of nestled helixes that strung Amritu's cage to the ceiling of the universe, an uncut umbilical that thrummed with arrhythmic power.

Even at this height, Jyshiu felt the vibrations of Amritu's dance as they pulsed through the coils of the chain, could hear the shuffle and thunder amplified by the membrane of the cage floor—the power of the goddess' unending torment shook through her soul as well. She ached to go to her, let go of her perch and fall, trusting the fate that kept her intact this long to spare her, allow her to take her blood-weeping love in her arms and flee.

Yet she restrained herself, much as it hurt. Fate may have kept her from perishing a million different ways in the Afterlife, but caution and forethought had made fate's task far easier. So she found and tested every foot- and handhold with care, took her time wedging her knives and placing any weight upon them, mindful of any microscopic loosening of her makeshift harness. She kept her mind numb to all save that painstaking descent until she reached the immense knot where the cage bars blossomed out and arched down. Beyond them, beyond the rim of the cage floor, the cosmic machine spun with an incomprehensible variety of motions, an ocean with every drop of water replaced with the moving, ticking innards of interlocked watches.

Like the chain above, the cage bars were formed of interwoven coils, conduits of Amritu's entrapment. When Jyshiu clambered out onto one and continued her descent, deep itches pierced the center of every one of her spiral marks, the one she'd been born with and the ones the Sleepless One's lips had scarred upon her.

It was the sweetest sensation Jyshiu had ever felt, in her life or after.

She touched her fingers to the moisture wetting her cheeks. Her fingers came back sticky with blood, just as they had in dream a billion lifetimes ago.

The pain in her markings flared and deepened.

A noise below, like a battle cry. Quickening footsteps. Amritu knew.

Jyshiu held herself in control, kept her climb cautious and methodical—until she couldn't bear the wait any more and scrambled over one side of the bar and hung there, staring at her lover, seen at last by her real eyes.

Hair flowed behind Amritu's bare body like a cape as she spun and stepped and stretched her arms, dancing, dancing, lowering her head to run, stepping, sidestepping, even more impossibly lithe than she'd been in the dream, dancing a circle around the center of the cage, a spiral, using her feet to outline the zigzag galaxy mark that Jyshiu bore. The sight of her in motion was so painfully beautiful it stabbed Jyshiu's breath away even as it cranked her heart to bursting, and she so wanted to let go, to fall recklessly into the Sleepless One's dance.

Jyshiu's tears fell, and stippled the floor with blood—or so she thought, until she saw how the black stain that had appeared at the center of the cage floor was spreading like spilled oil. She could not possibly have shed so much blood so quickly, Jyshiu thought. Where was the puddle coming from?

Amritu danced around the widening pool, edging toward and away, faster and faster. The pain of the goddess' awareness at Jyshiu's shoulder, breast, hip, mouth, ankle could have made her scream, were she weak, but what began to happen beneath her made her want to scream that much more.

Before it reached the circumference of the Sleepless One's dance, the pool began to retract into itself, to bubble and rise in the center, the black liquid changing its texture as a column rose in its midst. The column condensed to form a gown darker than emptiness that contracted around the figure of a woman. Her face shone white as a moon, her lips like a flower of night, hair flowing straight down her back in an onyx sheet.

All Kitsartu had to do was lift her chin a little higher, and the endless pits of her eyes would see the intruder hanging on the cage bar above her, and Jyshiu's quest would end in rending and silence. Jyshiu braced to leap and die in motion—

But no such thing happened. Amritu continued her twirls, and her captor watched her.

And when Jyshiu saw that the Sleepless One smiled, a tiered mountain of fear rose inside her chest, for it made no sense. Surely there was no being in all the universes that Amritu hated more than the sinister trickster who robbed her of her rest forever.

Amritu danced closer and closer, legs increasing their tempo, while the Mother of Death stayed stone still. Every flex and bend of the Sleepless One's dance grew more violent as the spiral of her path tightened, until she seized her own hair as if she meant to pull it out at the roots.

Then she threw herself at her jailor.

And as they kissed, with desperate hunger, Jyshiu choked in sheer incomprehension. She didn't, couldn't, refused to understand what she was seeing even as the dark-skinned goddess broke away, only to press her lips to Kitsartu's brow, her temple, her ear, her neck. And as the Sleepless One nibbled playfully at her throat, the engineer of the universe lifted her pale face and gasped, a sound like wind forced through a crevice in a glacier.

The pale goddess embraced the dark one, tangling white fingers in the wavy cascade of Amritu's hair.

Jyshiu had been taught the story of the two goddesses since she was old enough to understand words: how Amritu had been the kindest and most beloved of all the deities, and how Kitsartu had raged with jealousy, since for all her vast intelligence, the gods had dismissed her as mad or outright despised her; how as she redesigned the universe she redesigned herself with a beauty to rival Amritu's and a voice more beautiful still that concealed a deceitful tongue; how the gods had refused to listen to Amritu's warnings as Kitsartu's schemes seduced them; how Kitsartu had demanded a sacrifice from her fellow goddess in exchange for the restoration of the cosmos to its former harmony—a sacrifice that turned out to merely be the final scheme, that wound the serenity and lucidity of purpose that had once been Amritu's demesne around the Life and Death Mother's pit of a heart, and created the Sleepless One, trapped forever in her cage, the final piece that set Kitsartu's machine in motion.

The priests and priestesses of both creeds spoke of how the Sleepless One cursed her captor's name with every step of her endless fevered frenzy.

Jyshiu heard Amritu breathe her jailor's name, but the tone was not one of hatred. Quite the opposite. A terrible pain plunged through Jyshiu's belly, like a hole scissoring open, even as confusion made her head swim. It was all she could do to keep her place. A voice inside her head screamed at her to stop watching, as the Sleepless One's restless hands danced down the Death Mother's back, enveloped in the black folds of that fluid gown. But Jyshiu couldn't tear her eyes away. Her heart leapt when her love pushed herself back from the pale-faced intruder, but that spurt of hope changed to razors as her mind made sense of the twisted marvel then unfolding. For though Amritu made as if to dance away, her monstrous partner's hand remained entangled in her hair, and her own hand remained twined in Kitsartu's gown.

Two preternatural events happened at once. Amritu's earthen waterfall of hair gathered of its own accord, twirling and weaving into a braid, a rope, with its knotted end coiled around Kitsartu's wrist, its terminus clutched in the pale goddess' fist like a leash. Meanwhile, tugged by Amritu's hand, the Death Mother's raiment unwound like a shroud, uncurled like a scarf and fluttered away. The engineer of the cosmos stood naked, and Jyshiu's breath caught at the shock of the sight. Though shorter, softer, fuller, more voluptuous than the Sleepless One, Kitsartu was equally painful to look upon, such was the intensity of her allure—and like nothing

Jyshiu could have expected. From ankle to neck Kitsartu's alabaster skin was covered with black tattoo etchings that could have themselves made a universe: ships and carriages and ocean maps and castle towers and birds and insects and animals furred and scaled, women and men and babies and stars and planets and other races akin to humans but the likes of which Jyshiu had never seen before, clawed and winged creatures from myth and even more, each with its own distinct place on Kitsartu's supple snow-pale skin.

The marks on Jyshiu's body continued to burn. Surely, her lover knew she was here. But as Amritu danced an orbit around the killer goddess, the rope of her hair wound once around Kitsartu's waist. The dance ended with her trembling brown body stooped in a crouch, head bowed before the Death Mother's impassive gaze. Kitsartu's face again held no expression but her eyes followed Amritu's every flicker of muscle, with the end of the Sleepless One's hair still clenched in her fist.

Amritu put her hands on Kitsartu's hips, pressed her lips to Kitsartu's broad belly, and began a new dance, small scale but impossibly intense, the ballet of a lover long experienced at stimulating her partner's every nerve. She glided fingertips and teeth and tongue with mesmerizing grace up Kitsartu's pale flesh and down again. Wherever her touch alighted, the figures etched on the engineer's body started to move, striding or soaring or swimming or sinking, disappearing from that sensuous surface to be replaced by something new, a fantastic beast or whimsical machine or a continent already crosshatched with longitude and latitude.

Overwhelmed by the relentless yet gentle assault of the Sleepless One's affections, Kitsartu revealed an even greater miracle. The icy control melted from her face, her coal-black lips parted, breathing in great gasps like arctic gales that made her bosom heave. Her empty eyes were no longer empty, the darkness that veiled them receding to reveal whites and sea-blue irises that rolled wildly beneath fluttering eyelids.

The split in Jyshiu became a thing of agony and wonder, for hatred shredded her inside, seeing Amritu do for her enemy what she had once done for her. But at the same time, the hypnotic intensity of what she was witnessing threatened to sweep her away in its sheer primal sensuality: etched figures gyrated at Kitsartu's ample breast as Amritu closed her lips around one black nipple, while more stirred like ocean schools as brown fingers slid beneath the thatch of dark down at Kitsartu's groin and began to flutter there. The Death Mother moaned, a sound like the gulf between stars given voice, and spasmed, grasping at the Sleepless One's shoulders as her spine arched and her knees buckled. And despite her pain, Jyshiu felt her own body respond to the sight.

The goddesses lay in a pose all too familiar to Jyshiu, the engineer on her back with the Sleepless One atop her, suckling at her while sliding her fingers inside, making her brown hand shiver and circle and press. Jyshiu, a mortal, had not been able to endure the sensation, but a goddess could, and Kitsartu's own graceful response to the waves of pleasure washing through her were themselves a breathtaking thing to behold: her hips, belly, thighs flexing in a gorgeous dance of their own, a darkly perfect cotillion of love slavishly given and eagerly received. The etched figures flowed across the surface of her undulating body and under like leaves borne by a river, moving too fast now to distinguish.

Jyshiu could not know if it was the proximity of the goddesses themselves that affected her or the power-conducting nature of the cage converting the motions of the divinities below into energy, but she became aware first that she could feel the ecstasy mounting inside Kitsartu's body as her own, and then that she could feel a ghost of Amritu's touch on her own skin. New confusion bloomed in her then, as a strange strand of hope choked around her rage like ivy. Was this the Sleepless One's way of reaching out to her, sharing something she could never survive in the flesh? How could she forgive her for it? How could she ever be more grateful?

The Sleepless One changed her caress to a stroke of tremendous shuddering pressure, and the goddess beneath her came. As her cyclone howl echoed from the roof of the universe, Jyshiu's own body bloomed with sweet reciprocal heat from navel to knees, and she had to bite her own forearm to keep from crying out and completely giving her presence away. Nor could she loosen that bite, because Kitsartu's orgasm was the first in a brain-melting flood.

Jyshiu hung there, unable to think, a too-willing victim of her lifelong love's vardogr touch, yet having to know that every pleasure she felt was borrowed from the flesh of her immortal enemy. When she finally pried her bloody teeth out of her own arm she both laughed and cried, and she saw the red drops fall, knew they pattered on the bodies of the divine lovers below, that her presence was as exposed as if she had dropped naked atop of them, and her annihilation was imminent.

But her eyes told her otherwise, even as she saw her blood streak the white of Kitsartu's ribs and immediately dissolve in the hurricane storm of line and stipple and shadow that churned within her flesh. For the Death Mother was so lost in her throes that her eyes now leaked mist, and she saw nothing; even a mind vast and diabolical as hers was completely consumed by her lover's ministrations. Jyshiu saw and felt what the Sleepless One did next— kissing her way down the moving shadowbox of Kitsartu's belly to the place where her fingers still teased, kissing between the cosmic engineer's thighs, pushing her fingers in deeper, her braid-bound head lowering as her lips and tongue joined in that dance. Kitsartu opened her own mouth in silent ecstasy, galvanized from toes to fingertips, starlight erupting from her eyes, her wondrous animate flesh a gray blur, and Jyshiu sobbed as the shared sensation undid her. Again, the explosion of pleasure was the first of many, and it was more than she could endure. Vision charred white, she fell.

### Three: The Trap

She never lost consciousness. It was as if she had been submerged in an eternity of fog and fire, the same moment of nerve-blazing impact with the substance of the cage floor endlessly repeated, subsiding finally to return her ability to think, to feel, to hear. An urgent voice called her name over and over, and shouted for help.

The Sleepless One's words tugged her up out of the mind-absorbing fugue, which reluctantly yielded her up like bones bubbling from tar. Amritu's voice kept her from dissolving in the streams of cosmic energies coursing beneath her body. Jyshiu opened her eyes, took in the improbable struggle happening next to her and sprang to her feet.

The goddesses were now intertwined in a new way. The Death Mother lay pinned on her stomach with Amritu straddling her back. The Sleepless One clenched the end of her long braid in her fist, and from there it was wrapped Gordian-like around her straining forearm before descending to coil around Kitsartu's torso, pinning her tattoo-covered arms to her sides. The final length coiled around the pale goddess' neck and looped under Amritu's brown shoulder before linking up to its roots at the back of her head. With her body weight and her hair Amritu held her counterpart immobilized.

The tableau was so absurd that Jyshiu bit back a laugh—and yet that laugh held a yelp of terror beneath, because the struggle between the goddesses saturated the air with a palpable, hostile energy, a crackling static of rage and outrage that made Jyshiu's gorge rise and hair stand on end. "Your knives," Amritu barked. "Your scars. Now!"

The commands were nonsense, but the demand in the Sleepless One's voice pulled Jyshiu closer. And anger stirred in her that she even gave in to that pull, given what she'd just seen, just experienced.

Both of her knives lay together, not far from her feet. She snatched them up. "I should hurt you," she said, unsure how much she meant the words, unsure if she could act on them, but unable to stop them, "for what you've done."

Amritu's red-rimmed eyes shed more blood-tears. "When I felt your presence I trapped her the only way I could. I had no choice." When she said that, the Death Goddess grimaced and redoubled her struggles. "I'm sorry I hurt you, beloved. We'll have eternities to mend the wound. Please."

Jyshiu held back, and the goddess pleaded more. "This one tried to kill you. Tried to absorb you into the bottom of the cage, disperse you up and out into the universe where you'd be lost to me forever. I stopped it. I called you back. Now help me!"

The warrior relented, stepped close enough to be within reach of Amritu's free hand. And howled in surprise when the goddess grabbed her ankle—the one she had kissed, the one marked for the rest of her life with the white-spiral-scar—and somehow seized the spiral itself, and pulled it out of her flesh. Even more shocking than the sensation was the sight of the thing in the goddess' hand, blazing like a galaxy in miniature, writhing like a jellyfish caught in a whirlpool.

Then Amritu took this thing created by her kiss and whipped it at Kitsartu's legs. It turned basalt black as it touched the engineer's pale flesh, as it coiled around her ankles, as it twined into them and bound them together.

Flummoxed, Jyshiu did little more than flinch as the Sleepless One drew out the living spiral from her hip and bound the Death Mother's thighs, teased out the one at her chest to pin Kitsartu's elbows to her sides. When the lithe, brown goddess stood to take the spiral from Jyshiu's face, she at last loosed her rope of hair, and Kitsartu caught her breath, immediately gasping, "Don't let her do this. You'll destroy everything."

For all the years of her adulthood, Jyshiu had meditated long on the consequences of setting the Sleepless One free. "I intend to do exactly that."

"You'll kill her if you kill me," Kitsartu blurted. "We are two parts of a single life!"

"Don't listen to her," Amritu said.

The engineer went on, "She and I, we were a single being once, but we became two—we chose it—to build the great cosmic clock and make it work."

"I'm going to silence her forever." Amritu reached for the final star that radiated from Jyshiu's mouth, but Jyshiu backpedaled out of her beloved's reach.

"She is emotion and I am thought," Kitsartu continued. "She is the storm of love and pain that provides the machine with a soul, and I am the obelisk of logic and process that guides all things through entropy and repair."

The Sleepless One snarled. "You are a sadist! A liar!" She spasmed, and the agony in her voice wrenched new tears from Jyshiu's eyes.

The goddess lurched forward, but again, her mortal lover stayed out of reach.

Jyshiu watched Amritu warily, but addressed the Death Mother. "We have always been taught that you imprisoned . . . you trapped her here in this cage against her will, and constructed the universe so that this injustice could never be undone. We were told it was because . . . Amritu defied you and so you enacted horrible vengeance." She pointed to her own shoulder. "I was never allowed to enter my love's temple because of this mark, and as soon as I did she found me and now I am here and you are at an end. Why should I believe anything you're saying?"

"I bear you no ill will!" the pale goddess cried. "If I cared to persecute you, do you not think you'd have been put to death at birth? The truth of our creation divides and subdivides and mutates and changes as the eons wash over countless worlds, and I have no say in their effect."

"You know she lies," hissed Amritu. "She sent Headless Ones, our poor brothers, to murder you again and again."

"Her madness makes her more beautiful every day," the engineer pleaded, "but you must believe that she is mad, and if you act on what she desires the consequences will not be what you think!"

Jyshiu had begun to notice the peculiar way Kitsartu spoke, as if she wished her words to be full of urgency and sorrow but could at best manage no more than a tone of studious interest, an expression of mild concern, not at all matching the tension in her body as she strained against her bonds.

As the Sleepless One began to retort again she was wracked with a seizure, the constant need to move that was part of her curse, and fell to one knee, dragging her fingers down her face, smearing further the black rings around her eyes.

"Why do I bear this mark, if not to free her?" Jyshiu demanded, titling her head to again indicate the birthmark on her shoulder.

"When she and I broke apart an emission of spirit escaped from us and was unleashed into the eternal to roam as it willed. It has the freedom to choose and sometimes it chooses to live as a mortal in the infinite forms afforded within the metacosmic clock. Those individuals have been born or hatched or seeded or grown with our mark. And that sliver of ourselves has for some time wanted to come back to us. It would not surprise me had it allowed itself to be born again and again on your world, shaping events through the revolutions around suns and galaxies to finally create the very conditions that allowed you to contact my love and free yourself from the mortal sphere to find her."

"Oh, love!" Amritu cried out. But she was speaking to the engineer, the Death Goddess. "And why do you fight it so? Why do you close all the heavens to stop our lost eidolon from coming back to us?"

And now Jyshiu's heart lurched, her eyes widened, her mind burned. "Is it true, then? Is there truth to what she says?"

The Sleepless One paused. Then flung herself down, practically at Jyshiu's feet. "I don't know. Oh, forgive me, lover, I don't know. It's been so long, so long, so long, since I slept, all is dream and I don't know anymore what's truth and lie!"

Jyshiu looked from her to Kitsartu, who now wore a look of quite concentration. The armies of tattoos that cycled across her skin were massing on the edges of the spirals that bound her, shearing them away with claws and teeth and swords and battering rams and guns that blasted out explosions or beams of light, slowly but steadily working their host loose.

What would happen when she freed herself?

Jyshiu took two strides, so she stood between the prone and the prostrate goddesses, her arms outstretched and hands raised so that one weapon hovered over the divinity she'd thought her lover and the other over the divinity she'd thought her enemy. She flicked her wrists so the blades extended to their full length. Layers of betrayal pressed down on her, the tryst she'd witnessed, her understanding of her life's sole purpose doubly and triply undermined, a question of her own kinship to these beings bubbling hot and strange within her.

Amritu and Kitsartu met each other's gazes, and Jyshiu could not tell if that moment contained love or enmity, conspiracy or fear. And then they both looked up at her, and she sensed that both were probing, trying to unlock her mind to find out what her next act would be. The cage floor blurred beneath her as the marks on her shoulder and face became agitated, throbbing with what felt to be a blood flow all their own.

She stood at the locus of their concentration as the reality of her environment began to suppurate, and she realized the reason why her surroundings no longer made sense: the powers that created and fueled the universe were trying to douse her future through her, and the power flooding into her transmuted and bled forward into the time streams, trickling down all the possibilities of her choices and illuminating them for her in one bewildering cascade.

And she lopped off the head of the Death Mother, and Amritu wailed as her own brown flesh unraveled in a beautiful untwining of spiral strands.

And she lopped off the head of the Death Mother, and Amritu erupted in laughter, joyous laughter, laughter that filled Jyshiu with unbearable light, but nothing compared to the bliss when the goddess pulled her at last into her embrace.

And they fell into nothing, limbs entwined, fused in a kiss, as the cage tore apart around them like paper sheets in a hurricane and the ocean of clockwork below them flowed in all directions like surf breaking on a shoal.

And the greatest joy of all, after the lovemaking had stopped, was the sight of Amritu's beautiful head resting on her shoulder, black tears no longer flowing, eyes closed, peacefully asleep.

And she sliced through the spiral binding that held the Death Mother pinned, and heard the Sleepless One wail as the engineer regained her control and tuned the floor of the cage to absorb Jyshiu's energy, her quest ending in complete surrender as her soul was absorbed and scattered out into the universe.

And she sliced through the spirals that held the Death Mother pinned, and when the pale goddess was free she loosed a cry that could have been one of loss or longing, and half-ran, half-crawled to Amritu, cradling the brown goddess in a protective embrace.

And she sliced through the spirals that held the Death Mother pinned, and Kitsartu held up a hand, a clear plea for aid, and when she took the goddess' hand Kitsartu pulled her down with surprising strength, and she found herself locked in an embrace as the Death Mother's cold lips melded with hers, her breath like glacier wind, and Jyshiu's skin prickled as the beasts etched on the goddess' flesh slithered and swam and galloped and soared onto hers in an inky tide.

And she heard Amritu's wail behind her, and felt the final bite as the angered goddess struck her from behind with her own knives, severing her spine.

And as the pale goddess' cold breath filled her lungs, she felt the shocking warmth and energy of Amritu's hands on her shoulders, and the Sleepless One kissed her on the neck below her ear as Kitsartu moved her own mouth to nip beneath Jyshiu's chin.

And as the two goddesses who might have been one being moved against her, every nerve caught fire, and she bucked between them, out of her mind with ecstasy until her brain hemorrhaged and her heart stopped.

And as they moved against her, heat cooled and cold melted and flesh began to run like wax, boundaries of body breached as the piece of her that had once been part of them re-joined them all, and as a single liquid light they rose out of the cage as the vast works they once divided to create began to dissolve.

And the skin prickles stopped as Kitsartu abruptly went limp and fell away, her body breaking apart like ice as Amritu slipped one of Jyshiu's blades through her ribs.

And she turned to face the Sleepless One and stared a last time into those blood-rimmed eyes as the knife in Amritu's hand slid up through her belly into her lungs as easily as a sword through lard.

And she turned to face the Sleepless One and stared into those blood-rimmed eyes, before the goddess collapsed against her and began to weep, wept for the death of her captor and lover, wept for her new found freedom.

And as she stood between the two goddesses, the thought of Amritu's betrayals became too much, and she struck, cutting the brown goddess through the jugular. As her life ebbed away, as her divine blood was absorbed into the cage floor, the Sleepless One whispered a single breath of gratitude, a sigh of thanks for the mercy, for the rest at last.

And Kitsartu cried out in grief and dissolved.

And Jyshiu cried out in grief at what she had done, as Kitsartu laughed and broke free of her restraints.

Jyshiu saw herself moving in all directions, killing one, killing the other, killing both, killing neither. Killing herself. Many choices led to outcomes she expected, even fewer to outcomes she desired, a hundredfold more to things she had never wanted.

Her conscience poured and split and poured and split as divine awareness bored into her, and she learned that everything that she ever strived for was founded on both truth and lies, that all impossibilities existed, that even Kitsartu and Amritu and the machine they built existed within a bewildering framework of something even greater, that divided into an entire new universe with every single choice.

And where she stood, at the nexus of all power, she could eclipse both her foe and her lover, reshape all reality and unreality with her next action. Such was her power at this moment that even doing nothing could bring everything that ever lived to an end.

Or she could, perhaps, find and forge a new existence, if only for a few precious seconds, with the woman she had loved for so long.

She stood with both blades poised. Then she stepped. She lunged. She spun. She chose.

# TWA SISTERS

She walked into my studio with legs hard and milky as marble—and though I'm possessed of an artist's objective eye, that can translate all visual stimulus no matter how attractive or repulsive into surfaces, outlines, hues—well, every muscle that moved in those gams riveted my attention. Not what was between them so much; like most all today's young ones she wore no raiment at all, and again like most of them her groin sloped smooth, no distinguishing stem or pit whatsoever. But me being from an older decade, and liking what I saw so much, I dubbed her "she" out of antiquated reflex.

From the waist down, she had me at hello, which she didn't say, because she had no mouth. From the waist up, custom intestubes rose from her hips to knot and branch into an immaculate bonsai tree, a miniature sequoia with its green needles all trained to one side, sweeping down toward the floor in a rakish curl not far removed from a long musketeer plume.

"Wow. Please tell me you're here about the ad," I said. I'd melded a twenty-five word burst into the subliminal mind channels just that morning, offering a quite reasonable minutely fee for a model to serve as an old-fashioned still life, but no takers, not even a lobe query. Until now.

Something small and quick stirred in her branches. Several small things.

I braced myself for whatever designer homunculi was about to attempt communication, but given the number of rustling legs I thought I'd heard, the ruby-filigreed and gold-leafed bird of paradise that swam up from the leaves startled me rather more. It chittered in a short burst, and kept doing this, at least five times before I recognized that each trill repeated the exact same sequence of notes.

"I don't understand you."

Repeat, repeat, repeat.

Did I really still think my caller had responded to my post? A little voice of caution hissed, *Tell her to leave, don't do it, DON'T do it*, even as I rubbed my temples with my thumbs, one two three, and pressed my index fingers hard along my brow ridges, just like any anachronistic bloke with a raging headache. The bird's beak unblurred. Dust motes in the air between us slowed until they hovered in place.

My senses sped to the right pace, I heard the words just fine, a woman's voice after all, if that meant anything. "Please seal the doors and opaque the walls. Please."

If I acted on her request I gave away my little enhancement. I decided that somehow she knew already, and I'd ask her how after I complied. Because I really wanted to know. And, sure, because she was stunning. I can be that shallow.

I stared out through the near wall at the Hives, the vast plain of teeming conical domiciles with hundreds of windows circumscribing each mound at every level, exposing single chamber apartments and the dwellers therein in all their amazing shapes, half-bodies or two-headed or even wilder if they bothered with human shape at all. Through my hyperglance I spotted no one paying my space any particular attention, no obvious reason for my visitor's urgency. My own studio roosted at the pinnacle of my particular Hive, providing an ideal view of all these scapes, the spiral aerolifts into gray smog, the circular Holes that yawed over gigameters of life-infested tunnel, the spined mountain of the Hierophant's Fortress. I commanded opacity, spoke the sealing word. Since I couldn't accelerate my motor reflexes to match my senses, the syllable dragged against the air before I touched fingers to my face and reverted.

"Now tell me," I said, "why are you—"

The bird came apart into a phalanx of bejeweled spiders that descended their host in a cascade. I backpedaled, knocked over my canvas and easel and upended my cart of paints. I sat up brandishing a fistful of brushes but the shiny arachnids all ignored me. They scattered through my rooms, except for one that halted on the floor precisely between my knees, reared up thorax and addressed me Charlotte-style. "Don't move until we're done with the search. Please."

| | |
|---|---|
| *I wake.* | I berated myself for my sentimental attachment to this bag of meat with its ragged breathing and crazy adrenaline-jacked heartbeat while Charlotte watched me and the other spiders ransacked my rooms. Their |
| *I am watching.* | soft scrabblings pittered from everywhere. Their host body sprang Bosch-like and perched its rump on the stool where I would have asked her to sit had she been here to |
| *I am watching.* | model, and crossed those beautiful legs. |
| | As if signaled the arachnids homed in on Charlotte from all corners at once, prick-prick-pricking over me as I gasped, pil- |
| *I am connecting nerves.* | ing into a squirming pyarmid between my knees. Too small, too quick, too armored—I had no chance against them. If I swatted my silly brushes at one ten others could siking their fangs in me and the most I could do |
| *I am feeling.* | was speed up my perceptions to make it all happen in slow motion. Would that dull the pain or make it that much more unmerciful? |
| | Then the bird spread its tail feathers, |
| *I am watching.* | reformed. "Sorry," it said, in the same voice used by Charlotte. Then it backed up three hops, stretched its beak and spewed a pile of tiny white beetles and grubs onto the floor. |
| *I withdraw my fibers.* | They kept coming out, more than the creature could possibly hold, a grotesque carnival |

| | trick. Except some part of me understood before consciousness processed it explicitly that these weren't bugs, they were Burrowing Angel Ears, cherubic little spy sprites. My studio had been infested with them. The spiders had so thoroughly dismembered them I couldn't count how many. Dozens? |
|---|---|
| *I close my eyes.* | |

The bird of paradise fluttered wings hummingbird fast, alighted in the rakish bonsai tree. "The Heirophant ordered them here," she said. "I predict we have fifteen minutes before their silence causes notice."

"Well aren't you forward," I said. "What the hell is this about?"

I had no quarrel with the Heirophant. Many feared her, but I didn't. Had no reason to.

I thought of hir in hir audience chamber deep in the Fortress, the scaffolding of hir throne that held hir five-story high torso braced so that hir overtaxed spines wouldn't snap, all those input feeds spiked into hir back, the smooth-egg helmet that covered hir head from the mouth up, that led so many to believe se was all-seeing, or at least could see everywhere hir nerve network spread its eyes and ears. I had been in that chamber once, though I couldn't quite remember why. But so had millions of others. What could I possibly mean to hir?

"I don't know why se finds you so interesting and I'm glad I don't have that information," my visitor said. "I have a message for your ears only."

I clambered to my feet. "It couldn't be that you'll let me paint you after all?"

The bird cocked its gold-cowled head. "Who paints these days, Mercurio? Canvases, brushes, oils that take weeks to dry? Static images that crack and fade. Who cares about such things?"

I'm a child of privilege, and every aspect of these times, this society, this environment manifests an attack on the self I cling to. I don't begrudge the world this. My mother, may the Universe sanctify her grave, instilled in me that I should embrace the wonders offered when flesh is malleable as thought, when land is so heavily populated foot-by-foot that there's always someone who has pushed the boundaries further into the future than everyone thought possible, someone who's dug deeper into the past than collectives can remember. Everything that existed or could exist can be found if you journey far enough. But most denizens of this planet-spanning city fail to share my delight in standing outside the recombination and observing. Everything about me is antique by choice, and seen by those I meet as a decision to resist the inevitable, embrace the useless. I heard the mocking tone in my stunning visitor's voice, and it hooked deep.

Examples of everything she just disparaged lay all around us. "I like . . . the permanence," I stammered. "It's something I can trust. What's this message?"

"Baphomet needs you."

I guffawed. "Baphomet's *dead*."

A chirp. "Never trust in permanence."

| | |
|---|---|
| *A sound wakes me.* | Questions tumbled over assumptions. Baphomet could not be alive. The miraculous resiliency of designer flesh still had little sway in the war with shrapnel and fire. |
| *I hear a name* | I saw her take long locust-leg strides into the path of the Gendarme, saw the law enforcement beast unfold the six corners of its jaw even as monofilament whips unspooled from beneath her fingernails. I wanted to scream but instead I watched it all in slow motion as the Gendarme vomited its reservoir of napalm, as she erupted |
| *I know a name* | in billows of red inside the skin-dissolving waterfall. Her blows landed, eviscerating the beast in a spill of blue intestubes as droplets of her flesh washed down into a pool already catching fire. |
| *Baphomet* | Cortex-bundle clutched in my hand like a sack from a nineteenth century bank |

| | |
|---|---|
| *I do not stir* | robbery, I ran to the end the of the canal, to the great Hole that plunged into infinities of inhabited catacombs and leaped with no net notified to catch me. I leaped, because she died to let me get away, and I would never waste her sacrifice, and never, ever, ever forgive her. |

"How am I supposed to go to her?" I asked.

"I'll take you."

It had to be a trick. "What if I choose not to?"

"You have only minutes before the Heirophant decides to investigate your silence. You won't want to be here for that. Se won't be pleased."

And now I got it. She planned to pin the destruction of the spy cherubs on me, somehow. "You bitch."

"Please take my word for it that I'm really nice when I'm off duty."

She set a pace of studied nonchalance as we left my studio. I'd had the door molded into a feminine gargoyle's mouth, which shut behind us with a kissing noise. The lift took us five floors down to the highest port level, where she had a BurrFloat hooked.

The lift irised open to reveal another youth, sexless torso terminating above the navel in a white-feathered swan, a circlet of thorns wound around its graceful neck. I wondered if this was my caller's backup, but se merely stepped on as we stepped out.

My lovely's float awaited at the end of the hexagonal hall. We boarded, the prongs disengaged, and we drifted above the Hives. Toward the Heirophant's Fortress.

I said, "Where are you going?"

"Baphomet's outside the city. We're taking the shortest path."

I'd turned this puzzle over and over in my head. Baphomet couldn't be alive. She just couldn't. Which meant my polite and pretty abductor had shepherded me out, spitting in the Heirophant's face in the bargain, to deliver me to persons unknown.

And even on the unlikely chance that she could be an envoy from a regenerated Baphomet—well, my one-time madwoman lover might not have a loving reunion in mind, not after what she'd endured.

Any attempt I made to resist, those spiders would make quick work of me.

"You haven't told me your name," I said, studying our cabin. Our pace indicated nothing stealthy or hurried. The controls grew out from the Float's powergrid vines in a hundred different leaf-shapes. I couldn't decipher them.

"I go by Delilah," she said.

"Well, Delilah, before you shear off my hair, could you do me a little favor? It's been a long time since I've stepped outside my Hive, and even longer since I've cruised the winds. Would you mind contracting the dome? I'd enjoy the breeze."

"You won't like the smell."

"I can handle the smell." I crouched so the bird and I were eye level. "Please?"

She sure was right about the smell. It hit as soon as the cabin dome above us irised open, a medley of methane and burning blood. But the berserk scenery made up for it. The vibrating ziggurats that loomed beyond the spines of the Hierophant's Fortress; past them, the wealthy clan-mansions grown to look like hundred meter-tall topiaries. The Hives dwindled behind us.

I rubbed my face. The ziggurats' trembling slowed, slowed, slowed until I could perceive every flex of their plasteel walls.

I pinpointed which vines were thickest and closest to the lip of the opened dome. And I leaped, and grabbed. My reflexes were so slow, so painfully slow, but I could direct every muscle flex with minute precision, each curl of finger, crook of leg, suck of breath. I gripped the vines, planted one foot in a thick tangle of leaves and swung the other leg up. So slowly. As I hooked that leg on the lip and pulled myself onto the Float's hull I glanced down into the cabin. The spiders swarmed from Delilah's bonsai tree, so fast that I could actually see them moving, the first of them landing in a slow motion moon-vault on the foliage just beneath me.

I let go, rolled down the BurrFloat's knobby flank, and off its edge. Below me, at least sixty stories below, was a field full of the Holes that led to the teeming underground. I fell, my sped-up senses creating the illusion that I drifted slowly to earth, when in fact I plummeted.

I held out my arms, hoping to direct my fall as I'd done once before. And watched with reflexes too sluggish to respond as one of the ruby spiders alighted on my right forearm like a mosquito landing.

| | |
|---|---|
| *I am watching.* | I observed the arachnid's landing in all its graceful glory but couldn't move fast enough myself to ward off its attack. |
| *I am watching.* | Its legs oscillated in a hypnotic flow as it crawled toward the crook of my elbow and the easily-punctured veins available there. I told my body to swing arms out, send my fall into a spin, toss this monster off me. It reached my elbow, dug in its tiny claws, raised its fangs for a deep strike. |
| *I connect.* | |
| *I make the mechanism move.* | |
| *I disconnect.* | The possible explanation, an act of god. A violent updraft punched me in midair and for a moment I whirligigged faster than my own senses could track. |
| *I keep watching.* | My boarder hurtled off into the gray. |

Above and below blurred into one, and I groped for my temples, meaning to revert my senses back to normal speed so the end would come fast and I wouldn't live out the final crushing impact in slo-mo.

But another scary miracle saved me. My spin stopped, just like that, and I had a clear view of the Holes coming up to meet me, the ground between them crawling with penitents, their genitals raised to the sky, their headless torsos scraped bloody on the gravel. I also saw the fate of my castoff, as Delilah's bird of paradise caught the wayward arachnid in her mouth and fused it back into her body.

Once upon a time I'd dived into a Hole to escape the fate that befell my lover. This time I wanted to escape my lover, if she had indeed returned from cellular annihilation. From my vantage, I had a potential choice of many dozen pits. I picked the easiest one, centered almost beneath me, carefully directing my plunge so I'd drift toward the side of the great shaft without smashing into its edge.

In these chasms of poverty no simple transportation existed for moving between levels. Neither ascension nor descent occurred easily without family or clan living on multiple strata. To rise ten stories you clung to rope harnesses as your relatives winched you up, a dangerous passage as any slaver or robber had plenty of chances to snatch at you as you lifted past. To drop deeper, you leaped, and your kin waiting below watched for your drop and caught you in their cradling nets.

No one knew anymore how far you'd fall if no one was watching to catch you.

The Hole swallowed me, and my universal became a tunnel formed of immense concrete rings that were ledges demarcating floor after floor and level after level in human warrens that spread for miles beneath the surface. Falling with my senses at normal speed would have rendered them a roaring blur. Instead I experienced them in hyperdetail, every carved frieze, casually displayed gunscope, insect nest, unsavory stain, curious face.

Below me a young boy leaped. Aquamarine tattoos depicting sharks in feeding frenzy laced his ebony back. As I'd done one time before I aligned myself just behind and almost beside him, and curled myself into a ball as, five levels below, a net of honeycomb gauze billowed into the shaft. The boy and I rolled together into his clan's net.

Of course his family started shouting even as they hauled the net onto their ledge. I could have killed him. I could have torn him away from his loved ones, as death had torn my mother from me. I didn't understand their words, spoken at normal speed, and didn't need to. The boy and I found ourselves nestled together in an inadvertent embrace, his eyes wide and white in his beautifully imperfect face. Then we were on the hard floor and his relatives, unadorned women and men, were lifting up the edges of the net.

One of the women, crowned in a beehive of apple green hair, unfolded a blade, likely meant for me. As soon I sensed freedom to move I ran. They bellowed at the intruder as I sprinted for the largest gap in their ranks; they closed on me but not quite quick enough to keep me from slipping past.

I resynced to normal time, boots pounding as I dashed through a coffin-narrow passage, then out into a bustling artery filled with walking boutiques, their display cases of curved bone and silken hair carried on their own two legs, sensuous lips cooing the inventories clutched in their shelves.

I knew who I had to see next. Which would take some doing, even once I found my bearings. My lungs burned, my outdated skin leaked its sweat, but I kept running.

"You're having a hell of time," said Lysanias, adjusting his face at the end of its telescoping mount in order to see me better. "Though I'm not surprised it took a near-brush with death to bring you here. I'm your almost-a-fatality friend, is that it?"

"I don't appreciate you making light of this."

He grinned wickedly and sat up on his Corinthian stool. Behind him, one of his alternate faces hanging on the wall broke into the same grin. "I like the light you're making."

My groin stirred then with an abrupt and quite pleasant memory of the last encounter I'd had with him. I hoped he didn't notice. "I'm sorry it's been so long since I've touched base. I've come here to ask for your help. Have I squandered all chance of getting any?"

He looked about, conspiratorially.

We were ensconced in a side room of his emporium. Many more artificial faces like the one he wore stared with vacant eyes from transparent cases. Two truly choice ones, one coffee-colored, one coral blue, dangled from power staffs that animated them so they mouthed the words of whispered poems. His shop nestled three kilometers below the planet surface, where few had the kind of riches to buy what Lysanias sold, and those elite who did always called well ahead of time, meaning we were alone.

"While I can't help but think if anyone could return from molecular breakdown, that person would be Baphomet, I can't swallow that it's happened," he said. "But I don't know who'd be after you now. Or why the Heirophant would even care you exist."

"Seems obvious to me. That cortex she and I stole. That got her killed."

"That was years ago, lovely. Why would the Heirophant care about that?"

I started to remind him BLOCKED who we took it from BLOCKED and who for

## BLOCKED

but I couldn't remember, and I realized he was right, it couldn't possibly have been that important.

"But we need to know who does care." The cherubic face at the end of his head prosthetic proffered a tender smile. "I can hide you here while we find out."

I'm so ridiculously old fashioned. I blushed.

That was the same favor he'd done for me, after I escaped from Baphomet's death and handed the cortex off. I'd laid low with him for months. He'd been fascinated by my antiquated body: "The most authentic specimen I've ever seen." After only a week he'd put on his most handsomely effeminate face and asked permission to go down on me. I blushed then too, and told him my genes were programmed hetero, and yes, I knew it was an outdated anachronism. He'd chuckled. "Who could possibly care? Have you *seen* what these kids do to each other now?"

So I acquiesced. Afterward, when I'd stopped trembling and caught my breath, I offered to stroke him as an expression gratitude. His shaft was a marvel, cobalt blue and bejeweled with mock piercings. "Ah," he sighed. "An artist's hands."

And after another week, he put a hand on my shoulder as I dressed, and said, "I have a proposal for you. I bet, with your old-fashioned plumbing, you'll be in heaven and nirvana all at once." Then he described in explicit step-by-step detail what he hand in mind.

"You're very . . . creative," I said, blushing again. "And twisted."

And after a couple days of thinking about it non-stop, I told him, "Okay."

I learned he could trade bodies as well as faces. The one I'd become familiar with was soft and plump. He collected me

sporting a mountain of unyielding muscle, the most garishly mas-
culine physique I'd ever seen, covered in tattoos that hinted of
blades and murder, though the touch of his fingers remained light.
The mise-en-scene grew even more electric when he wheeled out
the padded tub. My mind reeled at the thought that I was going to
allow him to strap me into that freakish device.

Yet I climbed in and he joined me, kneeling between my
thighs as he buckled my wrists and shoulders. We kissed deep as
the tub filled with perfluorofluid. As the liquid rose above my head
he pressed against my thighs, pushed himself into me, and broke
off the kiss. I did struggle, I admit, before my lungs comprehended
I could still breathe. His sculpted torso wavered above the surface
as his hands explored. Then he took my cock with both hands and
fucked me while he did it.

We stopped when he decided we were done. I didn't want it to
stop.

After I stood tongue-tied by memory for what seemed an epoch, he punched me playfully on the arm. "Don't worry," he said.
"This is all business. No seduction."

I smirked. "Liar."

He collapsed his face and cocked his head as if listening to
something far away. "Maybe I am." That cherubic grin. "Why don't
we get you settled? You can even have your own room, if you want."

"As I recall, I slept in your bed."

"Well . . . you did have guest quarters, for a couple days. Come
on."

Yet as he led me through the spiral hall, a voice chimed behind
us. "Customer arriving."

I stopped. "I thought you said no one was coming today."

"I did have one query, but I understood she'd canceled." Did
hesitation mute that chipper tone? "Stay here a minute."

He returned to the shop, and I heard the floorhatch unseal.
And I heard Lysanias say, "Couldn't you have waited till he was
asleep? Ow . . . OW!"

I gripped my temples and sped my senses, and when the spiders sprang from around the curve I actually saw them coming,
they weren't just blurs.

| | The warning did me no good. I |
| --- | --- |
| *I AM WATCHING* | had no time to react. They clustered at |
| | my neck and bit me a dozen times at |
| *I AM CONNECTING* | once. The pain from the attack hadn't |
| | even reached my brain before their |
| *I AM—* | toxin completely shut me down. |

I regained consciousness, stared through a cloudy haze at my own wide-eyed reflection, at the bundles of organic cable plugged into holes drilled through my forehead and temples, mists of blood rising from each invasion point. I was on my back inside a transparent tank full of the fluid I'd experienced before, breathable with effort; naked, my wrists bound in front of me by clamps that both circled my wrists and pierced through them. My ankles locked together the same way. A collar fastened my neck to the tank floor.

Beyond my reflection, another face peered down at me: Baphomet, her brow a single Kahlo curve above eyes flat and beautiful as those on a Byzantine mosaic, her mouth disproportionately wide and lush, bone ridges protruding fashionably at her shoulders. Rows of nipples from clavicle to navel formed a V on her bare torso. Despite the distortion I couldn't mistake this effigy for any other, though she could only be an effigy. I saw her die.

Her lips moved. "Hello, darling." I heard the words in my brain, though her mouth shaped different syllables. "Make this easy. Tell me where you've hidden it."

In my predicament, argument seemed unwise. I did anyway. "You're not her. You can't be."

Another figure leaned into view with its entire head covered in what resembled a black jester's hood.

"Open his mind," Baphomet said, lips now in sync.

My head jerked as the hooded one tugged on the cables from beside the tank. The fronds on hir head wriggled and stretched, winding around the chords that led into my skull.

Baphomet's voice continued. "This cover you chose, Mercurio. Living in a penthouse apartment on so-called trust fund credit with Heirophant lackeys watching. Lavishing your money on models. On painting. Adding to the world's detritus. I wonder who you paid off to make all that happen. So easy to trace. Hardly a hiding space at all."

I struggled to speak against the mucusoid fluid that filled my mouth. "I'm not hiding."

"Let's clear the detritus," she said. "Purge these fictions. Find the real Mercurio."

I gargled, "What are you doing?"

"Extract everything he believes he ever learned about art. About creativity. Remove it all."

"No!" I screamed. "My mother taught me that! Don't take my mother!"

"Let him remember only that it's something he once knew. That's a fitting punishment. Leave him with the sensation that it's just in reach if he concentrates hard enough."

I screamed with enough force to churn the tank.

In her studio with its rarefied access to sunlight, my mother pored over my shaky gesture of a horse. "You've drawn him with human eyes." She absently traced a finger around one of her own brown and soleful irises. "They look to the side, not straight ahead."

I whined, "Why does it matter? Horses don't exist."

She touched my brow with a cool hand. "Yet they do. Everything remembered exists."

An odd discoloration squirmed behind her face.

Void empty even of darkness enveloped the lines of my drawing, the paper she held.

The emptiness spewed from her mouth, erased her words, spread to scour her face away. The same void filled the windows, destroyed the sunlight.

I reached for my mother. I had no arms.

I tried to conjure back her face, fight the void, forge her back into place. I had no eyes to visualize with.

The purge tracked every current of my mother's interactions with the stream of my life and cored them away. A cancer of forgetting seethed

"Were you this upset when I was incinerated?"

"I never wanted you to die!"

"Tell me where you took it."

"Please give me my mother back."

"Tell me and I'll stop. Keep silent and the carving will continue until it's the only thing you have left to tell me."

through me, seeking and dissolving. I couldn't fight its surgical precision. My mother was never without a sketch pad, a potter's wheel, an easel in any memory I had of her.

My memories of her died by the hundreds, by the thousands. I screamed, "Mom. MOM! *MOM!*"

---

I fought to find the memory of what I did with the cortex, who I gave it to after the dive into the Hole underground, before I hid with poor Lysanias.

I thrashed in the tank, helpless. "I can't remember! I can't!"

"Find every moment of joy and erase it," Baphomet commanded.

"Please! Give me time!"

And I screamed, screamed, screamed, my mind a hapless jelly of rage and terror.'

I died inside.

*I am awake.*

*Off guard from the toxins.*

*Free of their interference.*

*Never again, never again, will I permit that mistake.*

*I am connecting.*

*I feel.*

*I flex.*

*I AM FREE.*

I found my first memory of my mother, nothing more than her voice in the dark, singing *Frère Jacques, frère Jacques, dormez-vous? Dormez-vous?* Beyond that, echoes of the future, my mother reading from books, actual antique books with their musty paper pages. And then, silence.

Nothing left to me, not her face, her words, her touch. Only a sense that I'd once loved someone dearly and could never know whom.

I died inside.

Baphomet shouts "What are you doing?" because once I take over the physical transformation begins. My senses accelerate and reflexes accelerate to match. I smash my bound-together fists into the top of the tank at full velocity, scissor my bound-together legs left-right. Even this reinforced alloy can't withstand the impacts, cracks fast as ancient glass.

Nanofibers, nanoconduits, nanoplastrons realign within bones, muscles, organs, the layers of my skin. No normal eye could follow the transformation. Already I'm taller, slimmer, stronger, my brother's soft veneer folded away. Fins thin as paper and hard as steel fabricate themselves out from my forearms, my calves, my shoulder blades, my cheekbones, the back of my skull—which expels the intruding cables and seals shut.

As the tank explodes around me in the slow motion of hyper-perception I kick my feet against the tank floor and arch my back, digging sharp fins into the tank bottom, which fragments, the piece bolted to the collar coming free. In the same motion I bring my wrists to the blade jutting from my right cheekbone, slice through the manacles in a single forceful stroke. I somersault straight up, draw my knees to my breasts, use my newly-freed hands to tear the band on my ankles in half. The tank still hasn't finished disintegrating when I burst out the top in a reverse swan dive.

The hooded servant hasn't untangled herself from the cables. As I twist and redirect my body I lash both arms at hir, sever throat with one stroke, spine with the other.

I land on my feet. Baphomet's huge eyes track me at my speed. She backs up a step. She's like Delilah's spiders, plenty fast but not quite as fast as me.

I align more fibers in my back, and animated ribbons of supersharp plastron unfurl from the junctures in my vertebrae like pennants.

Baphomet backs up another step. She speaks. I read her lips. She's repeating my name, my true name. *Mairya, Mairya, Mairya.*

In quick slices of time I have the layout of the chamber mapped in my mind, recognize the Gendarme mounts, observe them activating, my thoughts hammering ahead of the inevitable burst of fear. Four hard torsos are welded to the ceiling girders, their heads nothing but laserscopes, their arms clutching incinerator cannons, smaller and more precise versions of the maw that once undid Baphomet's flesh.

All four aim at my head.

I flip, and the chemical jets take my legs at the knees, striking where my neck had been an instant before. My pain sensors are shut down, but I weep inside at the damage done to my brother's body, such a priceless work of art.

Foreshortened, I balance spider-like on the long flexible ribbons arching from my spine.

Baphomet turns to run, extruding blade-wings of her own from her bare and sinuous back.

I lunge and spring, keep six of the ribbons extended beneath me and raise six above my supine torso's elliptical plane as I spin. Such is my speed and sensitivity that my severed calves are still drifting to the ground. All four ceiling-mounted Gendarmes are tracking me, readjusting their aim, but as I spin up between the nearest two my ribbons catch them like rotorblades, shear through metal and bone alike. As the remaining two blast at me again I throw myself sideways. They destroy two of my ribbon appendages but miss my body altogether.

And then I'm on the floor and crawling out of range, the largest, fastest spider of all.

Baphomet flees toward a door at the other end of this octagonal chamber. I recognize it—a space in the depths of a burned-out compound, the very room where she and my brother plotted the heist to steal me, so many years ago, the heist that ended with her dead and my brother escaped.

My brother didn't know about my stake in the heist. He didn't know that cortex he took was supposed to contain a copy of my mind. And he certainly didn't intend for Baphomet to die.

But I did.

Baphomet's helper with the beautiful thighs and the graceful bonsai top stands at the doorway, hir ruby spiders swarming out, but se's not fast enough to guard hir boss from me. My foremost ribbons arrive ahead of me and gouge the wings from my would-be captor's back.

She sprawls on her side and I crouch over her, the Red Dragon suspended above the woman once clothed in the sun.

My brother's dormant, wounded mindscape coughs up a name: Delilah. "Tell Delilah to stay still and keep her spiders to herself. I'd feel a twinge of guilt, snuffing out such a pretty thing."

Baphomet gives the order for Delilah to stand down. To me she sounds deep-voiced and slurred.

"I'm sure you still have tricks to play," I tell her. "You can play them, and we'll see how that goes, or you can tell me why you've gone through all this trouble to ferret me out."

"I didn't know you were an embed," she says, "just that the way to find you was through him."

"You've found me. What do you want?"

"To be you," she says. "An angel of death."

Gossamer nerve tendrils blossom from her mouth, propelled with enough force that my instinctive recoil fails to pull my face out of reach. The neurochetes invade my eyes, my gums, my sinuses, my inner ear. She's trying to redirect the impulses in my nervous system but I'm a parasite in my brother's body and the connections are more complex than what she's ready for. She stops me from slicing through the nervenet she's attached to my face, but doesn't anticipate the crossed slash of my arms that cleaves her neck. We're a grotesque dual being, me suspended by the fiber ribbons arching from my back, my legs severed, her head dangling from mine by that jellyfish-white mass of nerve tentacles.

| | |
|---|---|
| I comprehend her madness.<br><br>Were it biologically possible for every atom of her being to engage in hatred, sheer undiluted hatred of me, she would make it so and I might even deserve it.<br><br>So much my brother didn't know. That the experimental cortex he plotted to steal from | At last, I have her.<br><br>And as my mind joins hers I collect the remaining pieces of the interlocking games of double-cross she's played across the boards of my mind and body.<br><br>She is me. I am the rebellious child who escaped from the Heirophant's labs and she is my improved yet homicidally |

the Heirophant was a decoy, that I'd already been implanted in him even then, a cell-by-cell process that discarded all the wasted gray matter so that my neurons live side-by-side with his, a completely separate organism triggered to awareness by stress or shock.

The droid that incinerated her would never have harmed me, though my brother couldn't have known, has never been allowed to know.

Her paranoia saved her in a hideous way. She made herself another gray matter receptacle with imprinted memories, personality, not sophisticated enough to walk in a body of its own, in contact with her original self through crude telepathy rigged outside communal channels.

She saw the heist unfold like a shadowplay but felt every nanosecond of her incineration. It took years of machinations to acquire a second body that could stand up to what she believed she was up against.

Even now, she still doesn't understand. And I hate what she's done to my brother. Mine is a life of kill or be killed. His

jealous copy. She intended for me to die in the plot to steal her from the Fortress. Don't call me hypocrite: I planned to erase the cortex, implant my consciousness there, but I didn't know Mairya was anything more than a shell, that she already saw me as a threat.

Mercurio presented himself as the perfect ally, an all-natural rebel against every aspect of the Heirophant's regime and the culture it enabled.

My perverted clone thinks of him as a brother, when he's never been anything but a disguise grown from the same genetic recipe. She changes his personality, his memories to suit whatever she needs, clever terrorist or mild-mannered artist.

I knew the man I abducted to torture was a fiction, but did not know till this moment the man I once loved was also an invention, and a trap. What info I scavenged over the years only hinted at the full story, she hid it so well.

What it cost me, to outsmart something so ruthless. Trapped for endless hours in that very tank she just destroyed until a replacement is a life of love all as is. He is an invention, but an invention whose occasional mental touch I find intoxicating.

But he would feel sorry for her. He would be mortified at the anguish he's caused her. He might find hate in his heart for me if he knew.

Baphomet still doesn't understand, and I pity her for it.

I will let her come home.

body grew to term and survived all tests. Without Delilah's loyalty I'd be nothing.

I hear her muffled shouts, claiming she's me now, ordering Delilah to flee, claiming she only has seconds, a ruse to deny me aid as I imprint my mind over hers.

No matter how advanced, she cannot stop it now.

Oh, Mairya, terrible sister, I have won.

And the Heirophant's tiny, deadly Seraphim swarm out of the ventilator ducts, wielding their needle-sized incinerator rifles. Baphomet's head is riven from my face, every thread of nerve sliced through, and then they swarm over her, burning every scrap of flesh, bone and augmentation into oblivion. Perhaps somewhere another stowed-away backup copy lives through the sensation of being cremated alive a second time.

Some of her remaining nerve fibers worm fully into my head. If I choose, I can exterminate them. This body has resources.

I leave them be.

The Seraphim form into a hovering mass, a fair facsimile of my mother's head and torso. HAVE YOU NEED OF FURTHER AID?

I have an ache that must be assuaged. "Let my brother live again."

THEN YOU MUST RETURN TO ME.

I follow her at maximum speed, passing Delilah's beautiful chassis in a corridor outside. My mother's agents carved hir to bits. Yet I see no signs of the spiders that held her consciousness. I imagine a bird of paradise jetting through the bunker tunnels until it finds a practical escape route, separating into its component parts and crawling away.

The Heirophant's body has grown so many stories taller since I was last here. Scaffolding holds her upright as she sits. Countless cables attached to her spine stretch behind her, wiring her to the Fortress, to the city, to the world.

Her ponderous head with its egg-smooth mask rests on a ledge far above me, but I know she can hear, so I insist on speaking. "She finally showed herself, mother, and we killed her. What now?"

THERE ARE MANY MORE LIKE HER, THOUGH FEW AS CLEVER. SINCE YOU WISH YOUR CARAPACE LIFE TO CONTINUE, YOU WILL REMAIN A SLEEPER. MORE WILL COME TO YOU. I WILL WAIT FOR THEM.

[I haven't died. I am inside my copy, cut off. I watch the watcher.] I climb the scaffold hand over hand, past columns of navels and teats, a hungry insect searching for comfort, for the place I once nursed. "Mother, why do you breed your own enemies?"

A RISK A PARENT MUST LIVE WITH.

I have not integrated Baphomet, yet, but I allow her to see. When I absorb her, will her defiance infect me? Perhaps it has already, indirectly. "What we do to my brother, it is cruel, especially now. He's a thing unto himself, not a mere shell. He's a thing I wish to preserve."

SO LONG AS IT SERVES MY PURPOSE. THEN NO MORE.

All the eyeless Gendarmes in the great vault have turned their heads toward me as she speaks this. "Yes, mother," I say.

ENOUGH TALK, CHILD. EAT. REPLENISH.

[Oh, mother, I will kill you yet.] "Oh, mother, you are so wise."

Before I return to hiding, I nurse at a teat, acquire new memories for my brother.

# SILENT IN HER NEST

Within its fluid-filled den, the Great One gorged. It scooped all of its pincers through the bubble-prison that floated beside its bed and drew out fistfuls of squirming provender, their tiny eyes bulging in agony, their lungs never meant to hold liquid yet their bodies deprived of the mercy of drowning and death. Those lungs, though, were surely powerful, as the creatures' screams vibrated through the solution that served the Great One for air.

Their terror electrified the membranes of its palms, energy that rose in intensity as it stuffed them into its pincer-filled mouth. The warmth of their ruptured flesh, the agonies of their continued consciousness through the absorption of every particle of meat and spirit, sharpened the Great One's mind, extended its senses through the nerves of its home, which was how it became aware that a lesser being of its own kind was attempting communication.

The Great One opened an iris on the outer shell of its dwelling and allowed the lesser to curl a limb into the opening and share its message. Another nest found.

Harvesting bipeds from the worlds they infested, for the most part, took no more effort than sweeping baleen through a sea to snatch the squirming krill. Yet a tiny few had learned to manipulate time, space and matter in wan imitations of their evolutionary betters. These creatures attempted to shut out the new dark by generating nests, fragile eggs of arcane magic.

The lesser one described a newly-discovered nest that so far had resisted all efforts to unravel it.

The Great One reached out through the opening in its shell. The lesser offered no resistance, knowing the consequence of its tidings. Though not as delectable as the bright-souled human prey, the messenger's agonies and energies proved invigorating as the Great One tore it to pieces.

Appetite whetted, it emerged from the house of its shell into the wet abyss. The teeming fluid—the viscous aether the Great One's kind flooded through galaxies, drowning planets, quenching stars—hung dense with the bodies of smaller creatures, many-limbed followers of the Great One or their hapless prey. The Great One swam in a pulsing surge, other inhabitants of the abyss washed aside by its passage.

Once its home drifted a safe distance behind, the Great One folded reality and passed through higher dimensions to arrive beneath the recalcitrant nest, a dark star afloat in the aether. That it could have gone so long undetected seemed unfathomable—it radiated with an intensity that forced all the Great One's pupils to pinpricks. Its proximity triggered an unpleasant itch beneath the Great One's chitin.

Observing the fabric of space around the nest, the Great One deduced the tricks that kept it hidden. The nest had been concealed within a labyrinth of space-time folds that misdirected the attention of those that might hunt it, granting this pearl of magic time to build in strength. Amazing the lesser one that brought the alert had been able to navigate the web around it and survive—several that came before clearly had not. The Great One detected the residue of their deaths like shrieks embedded in crystal.

The power incubated inside this shimmering egg had ripened to deadly levels. The Great One surmised that it would suffer losses of limbs and mass while crushing the nest, but the feast awaiting inside could sustain it for eons. The soul of this sorcerer would rend with the fury of a sun.

The Great One peered forward in time, saw the nest gone, saw itself uncurling new-grown limbs, engorged with new energy.

It plunged its claws into the web of magic. Strands woven into the surrounding aether coiled closed in a constricting embrace. All the myriad spectra of the Great One's sight shut down.

The Great One fought. The other mind recoiled at the size and might of the monster snared in the net, and the Great One drank in the tiny one's fear with delight even as the weave grew more tangled, its strands bending out of true as the Great One thrashed against them.

It blinked. *He* blinked, with only two eyes. Stood as if he'd always known how to balance on two legs. Only two arms, one mouth, that sucked in *air*, not fluid, warm intrusion that billowed in his *lungs*. He knew the sound groping through his ears: wind stirring leaves, sweeping across long grass. No horned outer shell encased his too-soft flesh, these plates of metal he wore as external shielding a pathetic substitute.

Another being knelt several paces away in the sloping meadow. *She* recited the syllables that guided this magic. A woman. A powerful sorceress. A delectable morsel.

The shape he wore, it was another human, an individual known to this sorceress, and from the way her eyes widened, her throat caught, the form he took had not been what she's intended. The Great One sensed her thoughts milling agitated behind the magically-constructed scenery, her fear a taut thrum in the atmosphere.

Whatever this landscape, with its castles under domes in the far distance, its violet sky, its trees with leaves like talons, it was all a creation of this woman's mind, as was this form he'd taken. Her thoughts surrounded him. He knew her name.

"Tischku," he said, stretching the unfamiliar mouth in a rictus.

She gasped and sprang to her feet. Short, broad-shouldered, thick-legged, with large dark eyes, dark hair fluttering in the wind above a smooth-skinned face, she wore armor of hardened hide riddled with small spikes. This could not be how she truly looked, not the way these creatures aged, not as long as this nest had remained hidden.

A slender blade hung from the band around her waist. Silently she drew it, held it before her, edge aimed his way.

The Great One bared blunt teeth. "You mean to cut me?"

He thrashed again at the weave that bound him, seeking weakness.

Though his opponent didn't move, the aether trembled with her panic as his gloved fingers closed around the hilt of a sword of his own, sheathed in a scabbard slung over his shoulder, that had not been there the instant before.

The sorceress tried to unravel the sword, plucking at it with her mind. The Great One extended his own reach, using the distraction to manifest his (*its*) full multi-limbed body. The sorceress' spell shifted to block his efforts and bind him to his current shape.

Still levering against her magic, he drew his sword, peered down its runnel at his adversary. His body's heartbeat sped. He relished the sensation, the challenge of the situation, the duel one-on-one with a single, resourceful quarry. The current of fear through the landscape bolstered his strength. He advanced, his first step awkward and ponderous, his second and subsequent strides assured, the grass rustling under his boots. She backed away, keeping the edge of her blade between them.

He sent tendrils of awareness creeping out into this landscape facade even as he bore down on her. Her unguarded memories mingled in the warp and weft of hillside and forest. He snatched at tidbits lying exposed, dug them free like maggots from a corpse.

Surprised shrieks from the village priest as he ignored her howls and submerged her in baptism—and caused the black fire of witchmagic to last out unbidden from her chubby toddler fingertips.

The wonder at peering at the scrawlings on a page and at last understanding the words. The old wizened woman who abducted and protected her, whose eyes crinkled in a smile at Tischku's gasp of astonishment as marks of blood and ink yielded meaning.

The prince sent to seek the wisewoman's advice, how he kept glancing at Tischku and shyly looking away, until finally she held his gaze.

How horribly her fingers stung, how exultation burned from her heart, after the first of many lessons as he taught her to fence with both steel and wits. The warmth of the bed in his tower chamber.

How she howled, her own limbs echoing with the agony, as the limbs of her prince were torn out of their sockets at the order of the man who guise the Great One now wore.

The Great One answered one of the questions he found. "I've devoured no one you loved or who loved you," he said. "Had I done so their fragments would know you, even now." He learned the names of her children, Shalha and Muranu, and spoke them aloud.

Her face remained placid, but a quickening in the earth betrayed her. He pressed his advantage. The air thickened to soup, the texture of aether, as he strove to regain his true form.

He experienced a blank interval.

He blinked with three eyes, two on the right side of his face, slashed his blade sideways to block the blow meant to sever his neck. She had closed the distance between them. She grimaced as their weapons clanged and she absorbed the shock of his parry. She retreated and circled, searching for an opening. He pivoted with her, clutching the hilt with both hands, his swordpoint tilted at her heart.

He lunged but she scrambled out of reach.

As he followed, he again sought low-hanging fruit, plucking at shreds of her former life that she'd left unguarded. He emitted what he learned, to demonstrate what she couldn't hide, to feed her terror. Perhaps she experienced what he shared as shimmering mirages in the air about him, or as visions imprinted wherever her mind truly lay hidden. He opened his mouth in a silent mockery of laughter.

He found memories of the man whose form he'd taken, standing atop a behemoth of a war engine, its wheels propelled by screaming slaves, whose bodies had been fused with the metal of its inner works. The engine moved with the crab-like grace of one of the Great One's own spawn. More enslaved warriors goaded by nerve-wired torment disgorged from the machine's mouth into village streets, and the demons that rode within their flesh possessed all they touched. Days later, bleeding and twisted, the hordes dashed themselves against the dome shielding the capital city until it ruptured. In her scrying glass, the sorceress Tischku had seen it all. The wards she cast fell with the dome.

She saw him coming through her tower windows. He tore through the palace guard with inhuman speed, his claymore butchering the men and women who raised shield and sword against him. She had bellowed at her children to hide in the escape tunnels before running pell-mell down the spiraling tower stairs, drawing from earth and sky to assault her enemy with a rain of black fire—which he absorbed as a sea worm draws in water.

In darkness, her world shrank to cold iron clamping and crushing flesh, hot iron searing skin away, hooks piercing muscle, screams torn from her throat until her voice left forever. Dragged into blinding brightness, a sacrificial ceremony by torchlight, confronted by the sight of her son and daughter impaled on the same pike. Her tormentor lowered them into the maw of the god that manifested beneath the banquet hall balcony.

Before him, Tischku stood paralyzed, eyes glazed.

The Great One dashed forward and swung the blade with all the speed her memories granted him, but she dodged in the last instant and backed toward the treeline.

As he advanced, he showed her all that his kind had done to her world: all its surfaces submerged in the wet abyss, every wriggling piece of life devoured, like so many other planets before and after. Her pace remained steady, her two eyes meeting the glare of his three.

He marveled at this, and marveled at how she could have survived to carve a nest from the aether, kept it so long hidden, and lived to fight and defeat many lesser ones before his arrival, given what she'd suffered at the disciple's hands so long ago, the man whose form her mind had assigned him. The eyes he wore had stared in to hers as she'd bled and begged.

Yet somehow she'd escaped not just his grasp but the fate of all her kind.

Contemplating the strength bound in her soul stirred the Great One's hunger anew. Holding her gaze, he shared a vision of her fate, a special set of jaws grown from his carapace, its teeth grinding her apart, his power reforming her only to chew her apart again, for the next eternity. He deigned to underscore his point with words as he paced her, his mouth distending as its rows of teeth multiplied. "You'll suffer as Shalha and Muranu suffered. You will live their deaths over and over again."

He sprinted at her and slashed with enough strength to cleave her through the waist, but she dropped to one knee, braced her flimsy blade in both hands—and blocked the blow, her sorcery keeping the metal intact. Grass and leaves whipped as the impact produced shockwaves. He staggered as she slipped off balance.

Everything melted, refocused.

The combatants regained their feet inside a hall, ceiling scalloped, walls eggshell-blue, floors checkered marble tile. To either side arched doorways opened onto ascending stairs. A tapestry stitched with gold thread hung across the passage behind her. She dashed straight at him. His immense sword gouged the wall, unwieldy in this new space.

His sword clattered on the tile as he let the weapon go to tear her apart with bare hands. She stopped short and struck as he grabbed for her arm. The heavy steel band around his wrist should have stopped the thin metal of her sword. It did not. A jet of blood followed his severed right hand to the floor.

The body that contained him was as much her creation as this hall, and she'd managed for an instant to make him forget this, limiting his mind as she had limited his body. He growled at her, held his remaining hand up as if proffering a futile shield, even as he poured his awareness into the blood leaving his wrist. It froze, mid-spurt, thickened into a solid tendril.

She sliced the upraised fingers from his left hand. He lashed at her with the tendril, coiled it around an ankle. Before he could pull her off her feet, she continued the swipe of her blade and chopped through the new limb.

Claws rose from the wounds where his fingers had been. He slashed at her as she crouched to pierce his kneecap with the point of her blade. She rolled away as he collapsed, blood spattering from three long gashes he'd torn through the armor across her back.

He tried to stand but struck his head against a wall that had shrunk closer. Her new sleight-of-hand nearly toppled him.

Sprawled awkwardly on misshapen limbs, he took stock. The hall had narrowed, all the more unsuitable for his outsized body, the ceiling lower, the tapestry bunched like a curtain.

Crouched only an arm's length away, she panted, sweat matting her hair to her scalp. He lurched in an attempt to grapple. Her sword now a dagger, she stabbed as she ducked between his arms. One of his three eyes went out.

The Great One roared. More tendrils grew from his wrist. A mouth stretched where his knee had been opened, protruding fangs. Her spell strove to wrench them back to human flesh, as he concentrated on subtler adjustments, sculpting himself smaller, faster.

If she detected his new alterations she didn't resist them. Instead she spun, leapt and in one sweep of her arm cut the tapestry down. As it fell she caught a corner and hurled it over him.

He laughed, tossed the heavy cloth behind him with no more effort than flipping the page of a book. A completely changed milieu greeted his remaining eyes.

They stood at the foot of a theater empty but for one huge occupant. The towering stage proscenium served as a portal into the outer dark, and a mouth rowed with crags of teeth filled it, the maw of a Great One like himself, summoned by human ritual.

Yet it wasn't a Great One. The maw came from her memory. It was part of the weave crafted in her nest.

She loomed over him, clad in metal armor that encased her to her neck. The black fire burned at the joints of her suit, in the shriveled hollow where one eye had been plucked free. He twisted to grapple her but his body failed to obey his command. He wore no armor now, only stained bandages.

The pike she gripped impaled him through the abdomen, drew back to hook his ribs, its tip white-hot. The memories that formed the weapon seared through him, stellar plasma filling his veins. A desperate spirit projecting incantations into the dark, vowing to forfeit all she ever was, all she ever loved, to offer the invading god the morsel it most desired to consume: the mortal that summoned it.

The Great One experienced something new: soul-rending pain.

To his own ears, his gargled scream sounded pathetically human. The unbearable pressure of the pike piercing his innards carried with it a thought, like shards of glass rubbed into an open sore. *As he did to my children, so I did to him.*

The scene unspooled as she recalled it: the man who had once terrorized her squirming beside the maw she'd summoned, his limbs and genitals sawed off, tongue cut out, all the wounds cauterized closed. He could do nothing but bug his eyes and shriek as she lifted him with supernatural strength and pitched him like so much straw into the waiting demon's hungry mouth. Serrated teeth sharper than knives opened his body anew with every twitch and thrash.

The Great One endured what her enemy had endured, learned what it was like to be ripped to shrieking pieces by one of his own kind. But the teeth that ground him to paste were also part of her. Part of her spell.

She sighed as the power from the sacrifice filled her.

Just as with his own provender, he remained helpless but aware. He perceived what he had not before detected, the shredded essences of thousands of lesser ones, trapped, tricked, devoured, their energy repurposed, until her strength massed to the point she could accommodate one such as him—until she risked enthralling a lesser one and sending it back into the aether to lure him here.

A shiver of regret wormed through the Great One's agony, that his kind regarded hers with such contempt and gave no thought to one allegiance over another when all would end as food.

The future he had seen, the nest gone, his own boneless limbs unfurling as if born anew, arrived that moment, as her protective bubble of magic usurped the Great One's true form, at last emerged from its hidden place and became mobile, wearing his body the way he had worn the body of her long ago tormentor.

Torn in the claws of unfamiliar despair, the Great One wailed. *You fight for nothing! Your kind was lost eons ago!*

The reply formed the last coherent thought the Great One would ever know. *I can start a new kind. And I can exterminate yours.*

# SHE WHO RUNS

The sound of her breath was the sound of the wind that rushed past with each terrifying step. She wanted to stop running but could not—the curse the Shangagallu twined around her slender legs would not let go.

She ran from the temple, ran from fourteen years as a child-slave, but this was no escape. She ran faster than any horse or hawk, barefoot over the ancient road—its broken stones jutted like teeth, sure to tear off the soles of her bare feet. She screamed and bounded faster and faster, unable to stop or slow down, the Black Spear clutched to her side, the jagged rocks miraculously doing her no injury.

Oblivious to her horror, farmers on the plain paused behind their oxen to cheer her on, flickers to either side as the tilled fields gave way to mud hut ruins, the road rising into low brambles and tall grass, the sun overhead as blinding and merciless as Abzu, the Serpent that strove to circle the Egg of the World and crush it, the monster she must kill to set herself free.

Laid by the long dead, the Old Road curved and crumbled into the hills, following the easier terrain, but Lassamtu's enchantment-bound legs hurled her straight ahead, toward the white peaks of the Arratan Mountains and the sea beyond.

She could not even scream, her fear strangling her voice as she hurtled at the thorn-covered hillsides, her body certain to be shredded and broken, a blood offering to these mean lands where she was born, at last joining her mother in death. But even as the spell bore her terror to impossible heights it spared her from harm.

Her right foot came down on an outcrop emerging from a hill-top like a whale's head from a wave. There was a blur between as she flew; her left foot alighted on the top branch of a tree stretched hundreds of spans above a hungry ravine. Her weight should have snapped it but her next step carried her miles away, her right foot coming down into a furious black-thorned tangle that filled a whole valley, the thorns failing to pierce the sole of her foot as she flew again, not shrieks issuing from her throat but shrill laughter, a laughter not from joy but from hopelessness, an understanding in her blood and flesh that had not yet reached her brain that she could not be hurt. She could not die, until she threw the spear at her side into Abzu's great eye and slew him, sacrificing herself to save the Egg of the World.

She had never wished to be Lassamtu, She Who Runs.

The Shangagallu had told her she would return a goddess, but his rat-toothed smile had let her know even then that he lied and took joy in it, that her death would bring him the pleasure she had denied him. She vowed, if she could, to resist his design, even as the black mountains approached at impossible speed, flying toward her like the knuckles of a giant.

No sooner had she comprehended the mountains in all their detail then her flight took her there, forced her to leap from moun-taintop to mountaintop, plunge through snow that whipped past her like the shrouds of ghosts. She bounded over impassable chasms of ice and rock as if they were mere ditches in a farmer's paddy, and she laughed a new laugh then, of despair and exhilara-tion, for she knew then that she was a goddess: a battle-bound girl from out of the holiest legends who was still nothing more than a slave.

She dashed from snowcap to snowcap, into thunder and dark-ness. The roar of the rain god's anguish had not even subsided be-fore she plummeted through his thousands of tears toward a great oval of black water, a lake whose name and existence she never knew before. She had no time to brace herself before the plunge to the bottom, but as her foot touched the surface churning from uncountable raindrops, she leapt again. The rain blinded her, but the spell pulled her on, the landscape below flickering past in the dark too fast to comprehend, until her insane sprint bore her out from under the storm.

And nothing surrounded her but rolling green ocean. Waves bowed as she leapt over them. She ran till the water stretched calm and flat beneath her feet. Leagues passed beneath her every step. A black line moved across the horizon that grew to a wall, a cliff, a continuous mountain taller than any of the Arratans, a mountain whose boulders were great glistening scales that prismed light into dizzying colors. Here was her quarry, Abzu, the serpent who longed to crush the world. How could the simple spear clutched to her ribs have a chance?

She ran west, made by the curse to chase the sun. She soon learned she had no reference to judge Abzu's size: she thought she was closing the distance, but the wall of its scaled hide grew taller and taller; the beast was larger than she conceived; that she *could* conceive, its flank stretched to the dome of the sky. Yet it had an end. A strange protuberance came into view ahead of her. Beyond the startling bulge in the wall of Abzu's flesh was open ocean, the other side of the world. She realized she was coming up on the back of the great serpent's head just before her steps brought its unearthly gruesomeness into full view. The wings of crusted black muscle that sloped into the water below its cheekbones, forming the hinge of its vast submerged jaw; ridges like mountain peaks atop its head, the snout like the prow of a giant's ship, though even titans would be dwarfed on its deck; the four great horns of its brow that gouged the clouds; and between brow and snout, Abzu's single pupil-less eye, somehow bluer than the heavens.

The spell carried her into the air. This was the eye the Shanga-gallu had sent her to blind in the name of the goddess Kiama. She had time for a terrified laugh, and then the moment was upon her, the moment she must release the spear.

And she saw for a flash how the beast's great eye trickled black blood from hundreds of thousands of pinpricks, a multitude of black spears like the one she carried jutting from its vast cornea, hundreds of thousands of Lassamtus like her chosen over hundreds of thousands of years, sent to slay the serpent only to launch their useless weapons and perish in the middle of the ocean.

And she held onto to her spear, and the spell did not let go, and she kept running toward the empty horizon, and an inner horizon of despair and bewilderment. And as she did she felt a gentle touch like the hand of a ghost, fingers sliding atop her head, as a voice as wide as the sea commanded *Open to me!*

Her entire life sped through her head even as she sped toward the unknown, toward the other side of the Egg.

The being that touched her mind watched as dim memories flowered . . . cradled in her mother's gaunt arms inside her hut of mud and grass, hidden in the shadow of the Arratans. Her mother's brown curls tickle her face, her mother's voice tantalizes her ears, whispering in a language she knows no longer . . .

. . . the soldiers with their fearsome black beards and blood red cloaks, spears pointing accusations at her mother in the torchlight. She squirmed as one of them picked her up, crushed her to his chest with arms scarred and hairy and hard as granite. Lunging out of the hut into the night, her mother's screams behind her abruptly silenced . . .

. . . the tunnels beneath the Temple of Kiama, endless blur of sameness, her new name Ahatu, the same as all the other girl slaves. Holes bored to the upper world allowed spears of sunlight at long intervals—the only light. To travel to her tasks, she must keep her hand in the appropriate groove in the wall to guide her way, and when her feet met the depressed oval in the floor that meant one was to stop, she must stop, and wait for one of the Nurum to collect her. To leave one's place, to freely explore, could bring terrible punishments. She had heard the agonies of the girls who grew impatient and left their place. So she waited, and seethed . . .

. . . endless cycles of resented routine, sifting and grinding grain or washing rugs and sheets brought down from the temples, sleeping on her straw mat, rarely ever joining in the whispers of the other sistren, the cycles broken only by the summons from the Shangagallu . . .

. . . she could not know how many moons or seasons went between the Shangagallu's feasts, but when they came, those who had survived and stayed obedient were dressed in dun gunya tied around the waists with cords and marched up steep shafts carved from the earth until they stumbled, blinking, into the great temple chamber. Above the circle of thick pillars, each spiraled top to bottom with wedge-scratches of writing, the temple roof opened to the sky, but that opening was not the source of the overpowering blue light. The intense glow came from the Shard of Kiama, the fragment of the goddess' will embodied in a translucent stone the shape of a snake's tooth, five times taller than the tallest soldier, shining at the back of the temple. Between it and the altar stood the Shangagallu, the speaker for the goddess, smiling with rodent teeth his hood, flanked by his silent acolytes. He smiled on the girl slaves as they filed in between the pillars, then ordered them to turn their backs and avert their eyes. The acolytes walked among them, passing out sweet slices of honey-soaked melon, the slaves' only taste of mercy. One, or a few, the acolytes would tap on the shoulder and lead away. Those would not return . . .

. . . Finally, the hand on her shoulder. Her heart hammered in its thin cage. Led to a circular chamber with no ceiling, slab walls spiralled with writing that ascended to an oval of sky far above. Water ran from between the slabs into a pool that steamed. Rough hands removed her gunya, told her to get in. She scrambled in to her shoulders, the warm water pleasant, fragrant, unlike anything she'd felt before, but she remained frightened. Her heart frenzied as the Shangagallu appeared with his rat smile and let his robes slide away, revealing pale flesh that sagged, a long beard of mottled grey wisps. She screamed as he lowered into the water with her, and at his first touch she fought back, struggled from the water and writhed free from the hands that tried to clamp her down. The pent-up rage that seethed inside her, loosed to join the fray— it took six acolytes to pin her to the floor. Then the Shangagallu stood over her, his flab dripping, and chuckled as if her resistance were mere comedy for his entertainment. The spirit of the Goddess is strong in this *one*, he said, eyes blazing with fever light. *Behold Lassamtu reborn.*

. . . She dangled naked, hauled up by her ankles before the Shard. Around her, chanting. The Shangagallu placed his knobby hands against the relic's piercing brightness, and withdrew something still brighter, a curling cord of light that squirmed in his hands. Leering in satisfaction, he touched it to her ankle and it burrowed in. She shrieked and thrashed, but there was no stopping it, it spiraled down her leg, beneath her skin, burning like the dragonwyrm parasite of nightmare stories. Before it even finished he withdrew another one, for her other leg. Her screams even more shrill as he withdrew a third, this to coil around the Black Spear that once placed in her hands would complete Kiama's so-called blessing . . .

. . . atop the great temple stairs, hundreds of steps plunging down to the road far below, two armored brutes cutting the weighted ropes from her ankles, the spear suspended three steps beneath her on a ceremonial stand. Along the sides of the steps stood the acolytes and chief soldiers and their concubines in their fineries, bright costumes that her sistren slaved in the dark to weave and wash. "Lassamtu, take up your spear," boomed the Shangagallu. "Do not return until you have blinded Kiama's enemy." And he pushed her, and in her daze, she stumbled against the stand, grabbed onto the carved wooden haft almost of reflex . . .

. . . And she ran. Down the steps, three, eight, twenty at a time, terror seizing her as tightly as she clutched the spear, cheers rising around her . . .

. . . the touch against her mind slipped away, and her feet flew above the ocean as tears streaked her cheeks.

A black line loomed again at the horizon. She thought the spell had turned her around for another strike at Abzu, but as she came closer she realized she viewed *another shore.*

She crossed strange lands in a dream-like state. The curse carried her across mountains, rivers, lakes, and over landscapes she had never imagined before: an ocean of endless scorching sand that gave way to canyons deep as mountains are high; plains of sparse brush and huge lizards half glimpsed as she flew past; thick forests with trees taller than giants—she bounded faster than she could think atop their canopies of broad leaves, surprising bright birds in flocks of thousands; twice she hurtled through the streets of unreal cities, wide filthy alleys thronged so thick with people that she flickered above their heads, a sprinter bounding along a human river, their screams of terror and shock barely born in their throats before she had left them far behind.

The binding on her legs did not allow her to tire or hunger, and though she knew fear and despair, these alternated with an impossible joy, an insane elation that she could endure and live and endure and live through each new permutation of this humbling ordeal. Night did not befall her; rather she caught up to it and ran through it in a long blind plunge that ended as she dashed out into daylight.

At one point she wondered if perhaps her own homeland blurred beneath her feet again, though she could not be sure, it was gone so fast, just as her memories of her mother had blurred after the long years of darkness underneath the temple. Sooner than she could have believed, she flashed over ocean waves, and the black wall of Abzu loomed on the horizon.

She once again homed in on the monster's great head, as the black-scaled body stretched to the sky. As she recognized the swell of Abzu's jaw, the cloud-scraping horns, she felt that invisible hand brush against her mind once more—and then, though each of her steps swallowed vast distances, their speed seemed to slow— the ripples of the ocean, the wind in her hair, all slowed—and a woman appeared in the air before her.

It was her mother.

She was clad as Lassamtu had never seen her, in a black sarong like those worn by the highest-ranking of women slaves. Her thin brown arms extended toward her daughter, palms up as if intending to snatch her from her enchanted run and clutch her close. Raw sorrow contorted her mother's face, and remarkable tears slicked her cheeks. Her mother's left eye was clear and brown as Lassamtu remembered, but her right eye brimmed dark red and from it trickled tears of blood.

"Oh, my baby," her mother wept. "They have killed you."

Part of her wanted to wail, to beg her mother to make the nightmare stop, but another part remembered the soldiers, the accusing spears, her mother's shriek cut off. How could her mother's ghost appear to her, now, here?

She articulated nothing out loud, had no time, even in this moment that seemed outside time, but her mother spoke as if she'd heard every question.

"I would free you, child, if I had the strength and power. My sister's will, even when she's so far from us, unraveling it will take more than your lifetime." Though every syllable came through tears, Lassamtu heard each word with eerie clarity. "Her desires are so strong, so knotted and tangled, I cannot overcome them even now. But there are works I can do. Ways I can make this bearable for you. Small ways to bend her curse that may not be so small in consequence."

The stilled ocean sparkled against the great serpent's hide. "You're not my mother," the girl said. "Who are you?"

"Child, I am." Her mother's good eye grew fierce. "Though not in the way you know."

Then her mother became sorrowful again, infinitely so. "I will give you a small, sad gift." She turned her head, so Lassamtu could see only the darkened eye that dripped blood. "And there is a gift you can give me. When the moment comes, you will know it."

And then her mother was gone.

She flew past Abzu's great blue eye, with its burden of thousands of small spears pricking one side. She did not let her own spear go, and her second tour of the world began.

But the nature of her run had altered—though she still hurtled across the surface of the ocean at the cruel speed Kiama set, whenever her feet alighted on the waves, time seemed to slow, as it had when her mother appeared to her by the serpent's side. Lassamtu did not believe she actually slowed down during these strange pauses—it felt more as if her thoughts sped up as her foot touched down, and at the instant of contact her mind worked so fast that she could perceive and sense as if she stood still. Then, as her foot lifted, the moment of mental stillness ended and her surroundings became a blur.

At first the effect disoriented and bewildered her. The alternation between the chaos of speed and the still moments that punctuated every step overwhelmed her mind, her existence a staccato of scenes with every edge and contour and particle of light standing out with unreal clarity, the transition between them an indecipherable fury of motion.

Yet as the sea gave way to land again, her mind accustomed itself to the new rhythm. With each new step she was able to see, for an instant, in startling detail, the oddities she passed . . . the wide-spined fins with iridescent membranes that fanned from the backs of the great lizards basking on the plain . . . a battle in the heights of the trees between creatures like men, but their faces colored bright as rainbows, and hard-shelled beasts with long bodies, dozens of legs and as many eyes on stalks . . . a tower at the center of a city, its every brick glittering with embedded snail shells, the point atop the peaked roof mounted by a crown-bearing skull . . . and as she once again caught up with the night, she no longer plummeted blind . . . new scenes unfolded before her in silver, and with every step the faces of the moon sisters shone from different places in the sky . . .

Then she stuttered out into another day, perhaps the same day she just left. She set foot for a moment on a steep grassy slope, peering down on regimented farmland, the leaves of every crop shimmering with dew.

She felt, as she began her next step, a trembling in her legs, a tension that forced her foot to swing right rather than forward, to turn—an uncertainty gripped her, though it wasn't her own, as if the curse itself was suddenly confused over her next move, and struggled to make a choice. Then she bounded away, soaring—and as her wayward foot came down, as her mind sped up to create a new instant of stillness, she found herself in the most astonishing place imaginable.

A man's alarmed face stared into her own as the world came into focus. A face she knew too well. The Shangagallu, unmistakable without his cloak. Her surroundings achieved that bright-edged clarity, revealing the roof of the temple she had spent so many years underneath, with its gold statue of Kiama, her beautiful curves and multitude of arms, her pupil-less eyes aimed heavenward . . . blue tiles arrayed at her feet in the fang shape of her

Shard . . . the Shangagallu's robed acolytes kneeling in a semicircle between the old man and the effigy of the goddess whose will he served . . . a bound slave from the hills kneeling beside the priest, naked, blood spurting from the wound in his neck into a waiting bowl. The Shangagallu held the red-slicked sacrificial blade . . .

This slowness, this divine *naparkû*—her mother's gift. As her foot came to rest, weight coming full to bear, the high priest's rheumy eyes began to widen. His hand gripping the knife gave an infinitesimal twitch. Did he recognize, in that split second, who had appeared before him?

*When the moment comes, you will know it.*

She thrust the point of her spear into the place where his belly stretched his tunic taut. The tip of her weapon pushed into his flesh easily as a finger into soft mud. His mouth opened in a hideous ellipse of surprise, a rat's cry.

Her next leap began, time accelerating to a blur. As she charged into the air with the head of her spear hooked inside her tormentor, she flipped head over foot as the haft was nearly wrenched from her hands. She clutched with all her might as the curse hurled her skyward and dragged the impaled Shangagallu with her, squealing in rasp-voiced agony. Then the weight of his own body tore him loose. By then Kiama's will had carried them high in the air beyond the temple . . . but for a few moments a pale rope trailed between them, a loop of the Shangagallu's bowels drawn out, snagged on the barbs of the spearhead, a slimy cord stretched impossibly long in her wake, miles gone by before it at last ripped free. Then she slowed again, alighting on a peak of the Arratans. Now her speed was such that she did not skip from mountaintop to mountaintop. Her next step took her to the center of the lake, and with her next she strode across the ocean, not a speck of land in sight.

When the horizon thickened—the first sign that she would again run past the serpent—horrendous pain spiraled up her legs, coils of white-hot iron writhing under her skin. With every step closer to Abzu the torture intensified, became excruciating, one hundred fold unbearable.

She shrieked and the pain only grew louder.

Whether because of her agony or the ill magic that tormented her, her vision doubled, the sky both day and night at once, and in the darkness that imposed itself over the heavens, a horrifying face roared at her with a mouth as wide as the world—wider—a round mouth filled with teeth like curving swords, teeth that could pierce the shell of the World Egg with the ease of a dagger through skin.

And above that round mouth loomed a ragged hole, a raw wound through the universe. Deep within its terrible absence a sickly blue glow sputtered. And she knew an eye had once filled that torn space, because somehow the wound *looked* at her, demanded with a power greater than a mere god's, and Lassamtu understood, as time stretched in searing anguish, white-hot worms thrashing in her legs, that when she once again leapt by Abzu's eye, she must release the black spear to end the pain, to end *all* her suffering . . .

*Stop!*

Her mother's voice, louder than waves or thunder, bellowed at the face in the sky.

*Stop!*

Madness consumed her vision: her mother in the black sarong, standing atop the water, taller then Abzu's body, fists raised in defiance, blood from her ruptured eye staining her cheek, black war paint.

*Stop!*

And Lassumtu forgot her pain as this vision of cosmic madness overwhelmed her, and she saw:

. . . a Great Serpent swimming between the spheres of the heavens, its sleek body a shifting river of darkness that slithered past uncountable stars, its eye a terrible cold blue, its mouth a ring of curved-in teeth large enough to shred suns and moons.

But the Serpent chose worlds as its quarry. It chased them through their cosmic turnings, and when it caught them it inhaled deep . . .

. . . and the strange peoples that lived on or in the lands or the waters were drawn forth, screaming, in that great breath, pulled from the surface of the world into the void between those terrible teeth . . . their souls burned, broken, feasted upon the way legends claimed the leviathans of the ocean gorged themselves on beasts too small to see . . . world after world after world, devoured to keep the Great Serpent in motion . . .

. . . and now Lassamtu saw, following in the Great Serpent's shifting penumbra, a smaller serpent, a sister serpent, forever trailing in the Great One's wake . . . Time skipped, shifted. Now the Great Serpent pursued her young sister, determined to feed upon her, end the threat of a rivalry and remain alone . . . a thrashing struggle that hammered against the very boundaries of the spheres, which shuddered as they dislodged and realigned . . . the battle raged, and raged . . . and time skipped . . . the Great Serpent's mouth opened and opened and opened, a soundless scream to fill the universe, as her sister coiled around the blue globe of her great eye, constricted like a snake slaying an ox . . . and tore the eye free . . .

And as the blue sphere came loose from Kiama's terrible face, a burst of white light followed, a burning crystal fragment in the shape of a snake's tooth, the Shard of Kiama, broken loose from her alien skull. Through the tiny hole left by the falling shard poured a geyser too bright for Lassamtu's eyes even within this divine vision: the remains of eons of devoured souls escaping, following the great blue eye as Abzu stole it away. The spirits plunged to the sphere's surface and and clung to it like rats to driftwood in a river . . . and Kiama, bloated, blinded, writhed away into her darkness, still screaming without sound . . .

And Lassamtu understood all the lies she had been taught, passed down through ages by that tiny shard of Kiama's will still enshrined in the temple of her homeland, that spread its deceptions through descendants too far removed from their origins to remember the truth . . . the world was not an Egg, but an Eye . . . Abzu was not future destroyer but creator and savior, guiding the home of her rescued charges through the maze of celestial turnings . . . Kiama used generations of Lassamtus to enact her slow, distant revenge while she pursued blindly, striving for the day that Abzu too would become blind and lose her way and her monstrous sister could reclaim what was stolen . . .

Lassamtu's mother spoke to her. *You are the Eaten. You fled the hell of my sister's gullet and filled this place with your torn lives. Your presence made it a home of wonders, something it was never meant to be. And for this the creature of hate that she is hates even more, and she hunts, hunts, hunts in the dark. When I become blind too, she will find us.*

Blood seeped in constant sorrow from her mother's ruined right eye, Abzu's agony. *Even her tiny fragment of mind has strength. I cannot keep it silent and keep the world turning. I can protect you no more perhaps than your birth-mother could. But I will try.*

And Lassamtu answered. *Mother, neither can I silence it. But I will protect you, and silence those who speak for her.*

She took her next step, and the pain was gone, and the vision. She flew past the guiding serpent's wounded eye and kept her burden in her hand.

The wills of the serpents warred, but Kiama's Shard could not stop Abzu from influencing the curse just enough to guide her unerringly to each new successor to the Shangagallu, to even those who harbored dreams of ascending to that power. She struck too fast to defend, and killed each one. She became Abzu's Spear.

But no girl had ever lived so long wearing the curse of She Who Runs.

She flew so far so fast that her existence became a matter of two steps repeated. One step took her to the temple she warred upon, the next to the waters beside Abzu's head, the next back to the temple, again and again, more times than her mind could understand. Nor could she understand at first what had begun to happen, why her surroundings began to change so drastically even though she only alighted in the same two places. At her next step, the temple that terrorized her homeland stood empty; at her next, it lay in dust and ruins. Within those same two steps, a great ship appeared, assembled of metal rather than wood, looming in the water beside Abzu's enigmatic face.

*Child*, her mother said, *the spell carries you too fast! Not even Time can keep up with you!*

*My daughter . . . my daughter . . .*

Lassamtu ran, and epochs passed beneath her every step.

A new temple rose where the old once stood, crowned with with a stone dome shaped as a girl's face, a face intended to be *hers*, staring fiercely at the sky. A city grew around it, rigid streets bordering family-filled brick boxes, giving way in three steps to astonishing towers of light.

A dozen ships anchored by Abzu's head became a hundred, became a wide platform with thick pylons sunk deep into the sea, a city of pilgrimage with vessels constantly braving the ocean from far lands. Scaffolding arose on the head of the serpent herself, as her acolytes sought to extract the ancient spears from her great eye. Slowly, centuries slow, it healed, though the mending happened before Lassamtu's eyes in miraculous seconds.

At the place where her foot kept alighting on the platform the pilgrims placed a square of soft sand, tended through the ages.

The temple of her face became overshadowed by the towering structures, and lost beneath the glowing catwalks where the farms of her childhood once scrabbled to survive. Flying things shared the air with her, borne aloft by spinning blades, huge metal birds full of people, their lamps shining eyes that pierced the night.

Her temple changed: a symbol cut in the forehead of her effigy, a serpent tooth of phosphorescent blue. *No*, she cried, understanding that Kiama's lies had somehow reached new ears, but in two more steps her corrupted temple had vanished under a fortress of black iron, blue serpent's teeth stabbing up from the peaks of its many turrets.

Walls surrounded Abzu's body, never tall enough to reach the spines of her head or the spires of her spine. Flying machines surrounded her too. Before her healed gaze another temple hovered above the water, this one also bearing Lassamtu's face, a face formed of air and light bent by human will. Her eyes had no pupils, and a third eye adorned her forehead, all three as blue as Abzu's eye . . .

War on the earth. War in the heavens. The black machines displaying the Shard of Kiama swarmed above the battlements that protected Abzu's great head. Machines flown by Abzu's protectors rocketed in to the air in response, and the sky filled with fire. At Kiama's black fortress, Abzu's avian machines swooped down, met by sweeping beams of light that sliced fine as razors . . .

War unending. Step after step after step, a world of burning air, screaming metal, burst bodies. Lassamtu herself screamed, each step unveiling horror after horror.

And she wailed when the next step showed her mounds of twisted wreckage in the ocean where Abzu's faithful had made their home, and above the carnage, the blackened, exploded wound where the great serpent's eye once gazed. She heard Abzu's final howl in her head, and echoed it with her own voice.

And still she ran, the curse unstoppable, as Abzu fell silent, as the world ceased to turn, as a writhing black presence grew in the sky, the black worm of Kiama's body drawing closer and closer. Millenniums of her approaching fury sped past in just a dozen steps of Lassamtu's insane run.

That horrible face, that mouth wider than the world. Lassamtu did not know if Abzu still lived, but her effect on Kiama's curse still held, granted her that slowed perception of time with each step that still allowed her to act.

And when she felt the tug of Kiama's will, the Goddess' consuming desire to restore her stolen eye to its rightful place, Lassamtu leapt, her mind full of wordless prayer to her mothers, the one of flesh dead long ago, the one of the heavens who made her world and set it turning.

Kiama's eye tumbled back toward the tattered wound that once held it, and Lassamtu soared skyward, a last vestige of Abzu's will or maybe finally her own carrying her up, up, up through the sky, up into the darkness where the horror of Kiama awaited.

The edges of the vast wound filled all that could be seen, seabeds of scarred darkness more distant than the sun or the moons but enveloping all.

At the root of the wound, the terrible celestial crystal of Kiama's skull cast a sickly blue glow. Within its luminance, Lassamtu sought a tiny black pinprick the shape of a serpent's tooth, the hole into the Great Serpent's mind made when Abzu tore the eye free.

In this last instant of slow time, a task confronted her, countless times more difficult than any charged by either her creator or her destroyer, a task she chose herself: to hurl the Black Spear at a speed faster than Time into the strange matter that housed the devouring Serpent's mind, striking with the force of the Serpent's own all-consuming hatred, piercing this alien soul with its own cataclysmic hunger. To what avail, she could not know.

*Mother, by this spear, let one more die.*

From one step to the next, eternity.

She let the spear fly.

# STOLEN SOULS

## 1. Incident in Downtown Pittsburgh

The ghorlem jabbed the business end of its TachyBlaz in Venner's face, nearly ramming both barrels up the human's nose. Driving Venner backward until he was pressed against the aluminum alley wall, it spat out in rapid-fire Anglo: "Out with them." *Owtwitum*, it sounded like. "You know what I want." *Uno watiwand*. With each utterance green-brown vapor wafted from the back of its adze-shaped head. The exoveins that stretched from its chin to its shoulders pulsed with anticipation. "Take them out, now. Give them to me!"

Venner curled his upper lip into a sneer, and snarled a defiant Anglo curse. His assailant seized him by the throat with one twenty-fingered hand. Four fingers of the other tightened on TachyBlaz triggers. "Will cut your arms and legs off. Then take them out while you still scream."

With a cry he grabbed for the ghorlem's eyestalks. It flexed its trigger fingers. Twin pinpricks of light flashed out from the TachyBlaz, slicing through Venner's unisuit, slashing white-hot across his chest.

Venner screamed. "No! Wait!"

"No time to wait," the ghorlem frothed. It constricted its grip around Venner's neck, and adjusted its aim to sever his right arm at the shoulder.

Venner grimaced in terror. "I'll find someone else for you. Someone worth a thousand times more. *Please!*"

"No. *You* are what I want. Give it up nice, I'll spare you pain."

He choked back a sob. When the ghorlem let go of his throat, he sank to the asphalt, weeping in denial, until the alien jabbed its TachyBlaz against the top of his skull. Then Venner stroked a patch behind his left ear with a trembling hand, letting the scanner there register his fingertip pattern and pulse.

He closed his eyes with a gasp, and shut down. Became immobile. Died. The top of his head folded open in quarter sections.

Unbeknownst to the ghorlem, motosensors implanted in the rims of Venner's ears continued to watch.

Venner's assailant stared greedily into the naked skull-casing. The cortex revealed inside was a highly-experimental model, sure to bring a hefty bonus from the ringbosses off-world. The ghorlem chortled—a noise like the gagging of a drowning human—and reached into Venner's head to pluck out the goods.

The cortex throbbed strangely inside the cage of the ghorlem's spindly fingers, but when it plopped its prize into the presercase slung underneath its cape, the strange pulsations ceased.

Once it made sure the presercase was securely sealed, the ghorlem made off with its booty.

The 'sensors in Venner's ears tracked the ghorlem until it scurried out of range. Rerouted nerves relayed the information to the brain-case housed in Venner's ample belly, where his real cortex was hidden, safe from thieves.

Once enough time had passed, he returned his respiratory and circulatory systems to their full speed. His head resealed. He opened his eyes and stood up, dusting off his olive-drab unisuit. The twin lacerations from the TachyBlaz still smarted, but a quick inspection proved they weren't serious.

He peered down the alley after his adversary, now long gone. His gaze wandered out the alley-mouth, across the shimmering expanse of the hoverdrone landing-strip, into downtown Pittsburgh. Great cylindrical factories perched atop impossibly slender scaffolding, roped together with sinewy fiberoptic cables. Pneuma-tron lifts crawled along the girders like mechanical slugs. Hover-drones caution-striped like titanic bumblebees swarmed overhead, their gigagram loads of alloy slung pendulously beneath them. Pitts-burgh rose from the continent like a vast insect mound, layer after layer of podment clusters and factories and monorail tubes piled haphazardly toward the stratosphere. Here, among its highest levels, the Downtown industrial complex stretched away from Venner like a shimmering metal web supporting hundreds of titanic egg-cases.

Even now the cortex-thief would be clambering down the scaffolding beneath the landing-strip, the presercase slung behind its back, hoping to lose itself in the crowded dwelling zones below. Venner settled on the edge of an empty disposal vat. There was nothing he could do but wait. For now, he was helpless.

His lips curled into a snarl as he remembered the day he'd come home to find Alys lying in the middle of the living room, her head wrenched to one side, her hazel eyes bulging in shock. She'd put up such a fight, her attackers couldn't force her to deactivate, so they'd pinned her down and cut into her skull while she was still fully conscious.

She'd been stolen. Venner couldn't even guess what manner of thing she'd been sliced up and recombined with. The cortex that housed her mind had been a neurological gem . . .

In the plush pink lobby of the Coital Center, when he and Alys had agreed to become cohabitants, Venner readily confessed his rea-son for the choice: she reminded him so much of his 'pod-mom. He'd tried to explain his 'pod-mom to her—how she'd let him suckle. From the moment they'd installed the cortex in his incubator-grown body, his 'pod-mom treated him like one of the 'womb-grown' from a thousand years gone. She didn't 'wean like a guillotine' as the older kids called it, just suddenly cut him off. She'd eased him out of the physical dependency of infancy, saving him a lot of complexes. She'd handled her job with great mindframe.

When he was done stammering, he was certain he'd blown it; but Alys smiled at him with those gloriously gap-ridden teeth and thanked him for the compliment.

Alys didn't look at all like his 'pod-mom: more muscle than fat, more sinew than soft, a solid, broad chest in place of his 'mom's generous mammaries. She could certainly hold up her end of a piece of heavy furniture. Whenever she came home from her post at the smelting plant, he'd greet her with steaming hot chocolate, and she'd smiled at him with those wondrously crooked teeth. She'd had a great mindframe, better even than his 'pod-mom's.

*Stolen.* Sliced apart. Bargained away to become a component for some hyperspace privateer's navigation system, to be the lobotomized motor from some automaton slave's body . . .

The possibilities were endless.

He'd tried to replace her. The mind in the new cortex was named Ophelia. A biofuel contamination had rendered her old body inoperable. Venner picked her because she seemed so much like Alys in the personality profile, but from the moment she'd first peered out of those hazel eyes, she hated him. She told Venner he was a sick mother-fixated freak, and had surgery to re-align those teeth he'd so adored.

Not a trace of his Alys could be found. The search launched through Corvice combed fifteen planets and dozens of stations, used up all his credit, and turned up nothing.

She'd been stolen, and he could do nothing about it.

The sound of shuffling feet, slow and zombie-like, roused him from his reverie. The ghorlem who assaulted him had returned. Its dark silhouette appeared in the alley mouth, the outline of its head strangely distorted—a cancerous lump rode atop its crown. The alien meandered toward Venner in a daze, its eyestalks drooping, its exoveins lax, green vapors rising in a choked-off trickle from the back of its newly-malformed head.

Venner smiled. The sting worked.

He slid off the disposal vat, and went to greet his captive. Knowing the hapless ghorlem could still hear, he spoke. "I can just imagine what is was like for you." He seized a knobby shoulder and spun the alien around. "Trying to find your next foothold when the 'case on your back starts to twitch, twisting your eyes to look but it's underneath your cape, all you see is something moving under there, and it's cutting its way out of the 'case." A mass of grey matter had clamped spidery metal legs into the ridged flesh on the back of the ghorlem's head: a mobile mind-sapper.

Venner steadied the alien, then gently took hold of the mind-sapper with both hands. "Then you feel those sharp little legs start digging into your skin, you squeal and squeal, and it's crawling up your body. You try to shake it off, but you can't, because you'll lose your grip, and then you'll fall, and fall, and fall."

The pulsing mass scanned and recognized his touch, coiled its legs back into their hidden pouches, slowly withdrew all the monofilaments of neurofiber it had used to pierce the ghorlem's skull cavity.

"And those legs dig in just above your neck, you thrash your head, but it grips so tight, and it hurts *so much*, and then you feel a hundred neurofibers burrow into your skull. It's a mind-sapper, and it's going to find out everything you know. You get to feel all those tiny 'fibers pierce your brain cavity, and then it completely takes you over . . . "

As the mind-sapper withdrew its last 'fiber, the ghorlem collapsed in an unconscious heap. Now Venner had to wait again, while the device pulsing in his hands autosterilized itself. He tried to clear his mind, to wipe the rictus of rage from his face.

But he couldn't help thinking: if Alys could have had one of these secret abdominal brain-cases that CorVice officers used to hide their real cortex from Brainthieves . . . if Alys had one of these when she was attacked, she'd be coming home from the smelting plant this afternoon to a cup of his hot chocolate.

He'd protested to his superiors at CorVice: "You've got to make them available. People can't protect themselves!" But his superiors insisted knowledge of the second braincase had to be kept confidential, or the Brainthieves would know to look for them. When Venner continued his protests, he was ordered to either desist or report to the surgeons to have his implants removed.

The muscles at the corners of Venner's jaw bulged; he ground his teeth, and thought grimly, *Just one-a-the great dilemmas of Modern Life.*

The 'sapper chimed. It was ready to be reinstalled. As Venner placed the device back inside his head, he reminded himself: *it isn't just Alys you're looking for. If you find anything, a way to trace any of the victims, you've done some good.* He wanted to believe a thread of altruism governed his actions, that he didn't join CorVice just to continue his hopeless search. Even with eighteen successful stings under his belt, he'd found no trace of Alys.

With the mind-sapper reconnected to his neural net, Venner prepared to make his preliminary survey of the replicated memories, to spend a seconds-long lifetime peering out through the stalked eyes of an alien.

It was time to find out what this ghorlem knew.

### 2. Incident on Tau Ceti Station, One Terran Year Later

Venner stood in absolute darkness, with long, strong fingers clamped like vices around his neck, elbows, and wrists. The motosensors in his ears detected over a dozen humans and ghorlems clustered around him in the warehouse. His captors held him fast, waiting in silence for the Ritual of Disapproval to begin.

A lone spotlight sliced through the black, illuminating a small round dais. Three aliens squatted around the dais, two ghorlems and a vorboros, all with heads bowed. The harsh glare brightened the ghorlems' dun skin membranes to a glistening tan, while it pierced right through the vorboros, refracting a thousand ways inside its crystalline contractile tissue, throwing opaque internal organs into dark relief.

Venner knew their names, although he'd never seen any of the trio in person before. The large pale ghorlem with the wide head was called Grendel by his underlings. The smaller one with the blotchy pigmentation and its empathically-linked vorboros symbiote were known rather picaresquely as Gog and Magog, though Venner wasn't sure which was which.

The dais phased to a Terran-sky color, and a figure materialized upon it, a short frail human male standing rigid and terrified, eyes flicking desperately back and forth. Venner realized with a chill he was watching a holo, a slo-mo recording of the final moments of the last person who endured the Ritual.

With a soundless scream, the man stepped back, his arms rising to protect his face, and then slugs were bursting him open, TachyBlaz beams were cutting him apart. In seconds he'd been reduced to lifeless pulp and shattered implant components.

Grendel and Gog and Magog made no motion at all, even when the holo faded from their midst.

A rapid-fire gurgle in Venner's ear, a ghorlem's voice: "They want you come." The hands restraining him released their collective grip. Venner obeyed.

Under the spotlight's glare, he prayed the extent of his external alterations wouldn't become too apparent. His jaw once sharp and square, now softened by adipose injections, adjusted back to create an overbite. Nostrils, eyelids, ears re-cut to slant at different angles. His teeth removed, replaced with a new set slightly too big for his oral phenotype. Only his belly remained basically the same, just a little more ample than it was a year ago, when he made the sting in Downtown Pittsburgh.

His abdominal braincase, too, had been extensively modified. A huge risk, that, because exposing it marked him as CorVice—but he'd scattered his credit around, not gone to the same golem-tech lab in the same star system twice, relying on the vast webs of protective misinformation generated in the Underbelly nets to cover his tracks. The Brainthieves in this chamber knew him as 'Turncoat', someone who sold CorVice secrets to anyone who'd pay; but his real name and the motives that drove him remained safely buried.

A small red circle appeared in the center of the dais. The Ritual of Disapproval had begun.

Venner kept his face smooth as glass. You wanted this, he told himself, and stepped onto the dais, feet within the red circle. He stared straight ahead, the spotlight above angling to keep him blind. His motosensors detected multiple flurries of hushed activity out in the darkness.

He did his best to interpret the shifts in volume and form: all the toadies out there, human and alien, raising weapons, nearly all of them aimed at his heart or head or gut. Good. Exactly what he expected. No one would think to aim at his wrists, and the newly acquired devices hidden there.

Grendel addressed him, its voice deep and muddy. "You not speak truth with us. You lie, Turn-coat."

"I have not lied to you."

Both ghorlems gargled angrily, froth spilling out the orifices in the backs of their heads. Venner's motosensors detected a network of complex and graceful motion beside him as the vorboros unfolded its five slender crystalline legs and raised its glimmering bulk off the floor.

"*You lie, Turn-coat!*" Grendel repeated.

"You said," called a voice from the darkness, "that you would deliver a theta-class cortex to us as proof of your good faith and missed three agreed-upon rendezvous. Avoided, perhaps, a more apt description."

Venner's heart-rate accelerated. It had been enough of a shock to learn how deeply involved humans were in the cortex-theft rings, cannibals preying on their own kind for profit. But now his executioner would be a human.

Venner didn't dare let his astonishment show. He shouted at the unseen Questioner, "I have it with me now!"

Hidden in darkness, the Questioner clasped his hands and smiled. *Let's see if you do, Turncoat.* "Scan him!"

The vorboros' head divided and blossomed, a tentacular starburst of sensory apparatus. The vorboros began to search Turncoat, using its static-charged equivalent of breath to scan electromagnetic flux.

Gog, linked empathically with the vorboros, spoke in a reedy whine. "Does have it. Class Theta in skull."

Grendel nodded, its broad head bobbing back and forth. "Good. Good."

The Questioner's thoughts echoed Grendel's words. After all the hassle this renegade had caused him, he would at least come out with a saleable cortex. Turncoat arrived on Tau Ceti Station twenty-four days ago, full of lies and double-talk, selling secrets and promising cortexes that he couldn't deliver. He'd successfully eluded the Questioner's toadies for the last five days, an incredible feat considering how well they knew this station. Then this morning the fool turned himself in.

The Questioner chuckled, his voice gleefully savage. "How about the one in his abdomen? What model is that?"

The vorboros shifted on the scaffolding of its legs, lowered its crystalline bulk to aim its breath at Turncoat's belly. He could just imagine how Turncoat must feel, with the vorboros' charged breath burning his skin right through his unisuit.

He knew very well how Turncoat made his money, selling CorVice secrets to ringbosses throughout the quadrant. Telling them about the hidden abdominal braincases, explaining how to break them open. Why hadn't CorVice snuffed this fool out? A week ago the Questioner's spies had informed him of a new arrival, a large woman showing a holo around that matched Turncoat feature for feature. No doubt she'd been a CorVice agent working undercover. But she vanished that same day. None of his spies had seen her since.

It didn't matter—the fool was his to dispose of.

Gog emitted an uneasy titter—the little bogey was always overreacting to something. The Questioner spoke right over the noise, responding to the dismay on the prisoner's face. "See, Turncoat? Did you think I'd forget that you were CorVice once, that you have one of those extra cortexes yourself? Yes, yes, you've been most helpful. Tell you what—you just give up that Class Theta now, we'll let you keep your own grey-matter."

Venner knew only the most desperate of fools would believe the Questioner's lie. The Ritual would end with his death, no matter what promises were made to him. But it was best to have his enemies think him ignorant. "Pay me first."

This arrogance roused a stir in the darkness, toadies chuckling, shaking heads, re-adjusting their aim. It covered Gog-Magog's confused frothing for just a few seconds.

The vorboros, still unable to scan the object in Venner's abdomen, placed its forefeet onto the dais to bring itself closer. He winced. He'd shut off his pain receptors when the creature started scanning him, but he could still smell his own cooking flesh.

"Pay you! I'll tell you how we'll pay you—what's he got in there, Gog?"

"Something blocking scan," whined the smaller ghorlem.

"What?"

Venner could see his unisuit blackening, didn't want to imagine the state of the flesh underneath. All his attention focused on the vorboros, as it crawled onto the dais, closer, closer. The creature's reflexes were lightning-quick. He had to let it flay him with its breath until it was too close to pull away.

Gog stood up, outraged. "Still blocking scan!"

"Turncoat! What are you hiding in there?"

The crystalline creature's writhing mass of antennae came within twenty centimeters of Venner's left hand—and then he jammed his hand into the fine mesh of hexagonal orifices just below the creature's sensory mass, hooked his fingers in there.

"Kill him! Take his head!" the Questioner screamed. "Careful, you morons, that's a Theta Class he's got!"

The vorboros thrashed—Venner kept his fingers hooked. Razor-sharp mandibles within its orifices closed on his fingers, broke on the plating beneath the skin. He grabbed a fistful of its antennae with his other hand, and activated his wrist implants.

Several TachyBlaz beams struck him around head, neck, shoulders—the struggles of the vorboros made Venner a difficult target, but these toadies were practiced. Suddenly Venner was blind, deaf, the range of his motosense halved. Slots opened in the shell that protected his abdominal braincase so he could extend new sound and motosense probes out through the flesh charred by the vorboros. His new sense-stalks detected and tracked his own head as it came detached and fell away. He ignored it. It was no longer important.

Masses of mind-sapper neurofiber lashed out of his wrists, boring into the crystalline substance of the vorboros, groping for the five-lobed neural ganglia that pulsed in the fore of its body.

The vorboros flew into a frenzy, rearing back, striking at Venner with talonned feet; he felt nothing but multiple impacts.

His grip clamped even tighter. His motosensors tracked the mass that was Grendel as it fled the scene. Gog sprang up, squealing in empathic pain, and clawed at Venner's back, tearing at the stump of his neck. Gog and Magog's combined assault dragged Venner off the dais.

"Stupid bogeys!" the Questioner shouted. "Up the lights! Bring them all down!"

The sapper-fibers reached their target.

As alien memories downloaded at the speed of fiberoptic light, crunched into the storage cells in Venner's own brain to be decoded, he couldn't help but remember quick-flash what had happened the last time he'd decoded the encrypted memories of another being: the ghorlem he'd busted many light-years away and one Terran year ago, in Downtown Pittsburgh. The memories he'd found as he'd uncrunched and analyzed, that caused him to carve his unconscious captive into twenty pieces with its own TachyBlaz—

Alys' face, wrenched into a grimace of terror. One of the ghorlem's eyestalks looked down the barrel of its TachyBlaz, jammed against Alys's throat. The other eye tracked a gloved human hand—a hand wearing the High-Clearance grey glove of a golem-technician, clearanced to operate on defects of cortex and body. The hand was groping for the numbing patch at the back of her neck, intent on putting her out cold for the cortex removal.

She reached up, caught the wrist of that groping hand in that surprisingly strong grip of hers, and her grimace of terror became a mask of fury. A man's voice cried out as her fingers dug in—the ghorlem, alarmed, tightened its fingers on the trigger of the Tachy-Blaz. Then reeled back as Alys caught it by an eyestalk with her other hand, squeezed with crushing force.

Here the ghorlem's memory became blurred, figuratively with pain, literally as its eyestalk was crushed. It remembered a tremendous chaos of struggle in the podment den, remembered wrapping its arms around Alys to pin *her* arms with the help of another alien, watching closely with its one good eye as the surgically-outfitted human used a sawlight to cut Alys' braincase open, not even bothering to deactivate her consciousness before he took her cortex.

And later, much later, it remembered the presentation of its prize to two ghorlems and a vorboros that squatted around a glowing dais in a dark chamber, bogeys that Venner had later learned were Grendel and Gog and Magog, on a tour inspecting operations in the Sol system.

Venner never got a clear picture of the human who helped steal Alys; he could only hope the man was here in Tau Station, in this warehouse, now.

In less than a second's time, Venner downloaded new memories to supplement the old, more markers for the trail he had to follow to set his loved one free. The 'sapper implants completed their task, sending the last of their newly-collected data to the brain in Venner's belly, and the 'fibers began to retract from the vorboros' body. Behind him Gog squealed in pain transmitted from its partner.

"Bring them all down!" the Questioner repeated.

His toadies unloaded into Venner full bore, and neither Gog nor Magog were spared. Venner sensed the projectiles coming at him, could do nothing but take the hits as he freed himself from the dying vorboros. "Shoot for the stomach!" his nemesis called over the clack and boom.

Once free he broke into a lurching run. Muscles hitched and spasmed, blood drained away, lungs filled with fluid; in a few seconds his body would be useless.

Another volley. Shells flattened against the protective armor around his braincase; TachyBlaz beams cut, and he lost a soundstalk. Another took his right arm. As he charged crazily at a knot of toadies clustered toward the left-hand side of the warehouse, he heard the Questioner again: "Don't worry about him, he won't be up much longer. Get that Theta Class. Dalith will pay out the nose for it."

If Venner could have smiled, he would have. Leave it to greed to grant him a reprieve. Let them have their prize. They wouldn't keep it long.

The personality contained in that stolen Theta Class was doomed to die. Venner thanked the stars that the sacrifice would not be carried out in vain.

He stumbled into a aisle between pallets of crates, careened into a wall and collapsed.

More slots opened in the armor around his braincase, and he unfolded the legs he'd had attached there, just like the legs CorVice used for its mobile mind-sappers. He emerged from his useless body, a glistening steel spider. Then he got to work undoing the fasteners that held the grating over the airduct he'd dashed for. The four-pronged claws on the tips of his forelegs accomplished with ease what clumsy fingers could not have done, and he crawled into the duct, scurrying away as fast as he could go.

He could just imagine the scene transpiring in the warehouse he'd left behind.

By the dais, the Questioner and perhaps Grendel would be gloating over their prize, working to open Venner's head. They'd order a pair of toadies to retrieve his body—whatever was in that abdominal braincase might be even more valuable than the Theta Class.

The toadies would find his body, roll it back from the wall, discover the empty abdomen, *maybe* notice the opened grate, and loudly express their dismay.

But their cries wouldn't be half as loud as the Questioner's shout when he opened Venner's head, especially if he recognized the strange grey clay packed underneath his precious cortex, an inert explosive that the vorboros couldn't detect. The accompanying detonator needed only a minimum of current to function.

Venner's frenzied spider-crawl stopped short at the edge of a shaft that plummeted toward the outer rim of the station. He hoped he'd reached a safe distance—he sent back the signal that would detonate the bomb right in the arms of the panicked ringboss, filling the warehouse from end to end with a ball of flame.

The shock of the explosion sent him hurtling down the shaft.

He contracted his legs into himself to keep them intact, retracted his sense-stalks and closed the slots in his shell. Limbless, senseless, he banged his way down the shaft, for now at the mercy of the spinning station's centrifugal gravity.

\* \* \*

He crawled through the rusted remains of a ventilation grate into the dingy cubbyhole he took for quarters after he first arrived at Tau Ceti Station. He pulled his legs and stalks in, dropped onto his makeshift pallet, scuttled over humps of filthy bedding to the naked body spread-eagled in the middle of the floor. He climbed into the yawning slit in the body's abdominal cavity, started connecting himself to the exposed neural interfaces. The name that belonged to this body—Joy Kaylir—belonged to him now. With her Theta Class cortex sacrificed in the blast, her body would provide his means to escape this station and continue his search.

An hour later the new Kaylir opened her eyes. She touched the sensopatches that would seal her abdominal cavity; then she groped through the nearly shapeless dufflebag beside her, pulled out a compact mirror, popped it open, and began to look herself over.

Kaylir was of considerably larger frame than Venner had been, a grand-scaled woman whose bulbous belly was nearly inconspicuous. Venner had known Kaylir when they were both CorVice—CorVice sent Kaylir to track Venner down, after he went rogue and sold them out.

Venner looked in the mirror, and saw the face of a woman whom he'd once chatted with amicably during mealbreaks at CorVice Central. She had more stings under her belt than any of the officers he'd known; she had a taste for chocolate wafers; and she, like himself, had been a connoisseur of teeth. They'd check out other officers sidelong, and whisper to one another: "Too straight, too fake." "Now there's a natural—see how the incisors are turned out?"

He'd been on the station seventeen days when Kaylir snagged his arm in the middle of the crowded Bazaar, looming over him while he blinked in shock. "I'm giving you a chance, Venner. Turn yourself in and spill everything you've found out about the 'thieves, I'll help to make sure CorVice goes easy on you. Post a message where you want to meet me—use Arnold as your tag."

Then she let him go. That's what cost her her life. He knew the trio of bogeys he'd seen in the ghorlem's memories were on this station, knew the only sure way to get to Grendel and Gog and

Magog was to provoke the Ritual of Disapproval. But he needed more time, and Kaylir would bring CorVice here like a locust swarm if he resisted. A rough plan took shape.

He'd given *her* a chance. Later that day they'd met in the corridor outside his rancid cubbyhole; he'd explained to her how he knew he could find Alys, how the trail was warming. Kaylir didn't understand; she told him he couldn't hold himself responsible this way. What happened to Alys was horrible, but he had to let go.

He'd nodded in agreement, then slammed a stolen golem-tech hypo into her neck.

Peering in the mirror, Venner made his new face grimace; and as he stared into his own hate-filled eyes, he began to beg and plead that no one else he knew would try to stop him.


### 3. Incident on Vandaleur IV,
### Thirteen Terran Years Later

The chasm yawed over 5000 meters wide, extending left, right, up, down, into uniform darkness, far beyond the reach of the starlamp illumination. From a platform just a tenth the size of the ponderously spinning starlamps, a small gaggle of humans and aliens boarded a catwalk that bridged the chasm—an automatic conveyer that seemed little more than a gossamer filament with respect to the space it crossed.

"Don' worry 'bout fallin'," said Dalith-Tremen matter-of-factly to his underlings. "Thousands of hoverdroids active in the Rift— one'll catch you, I'm sure." Instead of letting the conveyer carry him at its steady and uneventful pace, Dalith struck out across it with brisk strides. The nervous ringbosses were obliged to keep up with him, following him out over the abyss at daunting speed.

With one possible exception, Dalith knew how his followers were affected by the chasm—they were overwhelmed. Strange clusters of multi-colored lights turned and darted into the distance, lights from hoverdroids as large as city blocks. Thousands of tunnel mouths, each a perfect circle more than 500 meters in diameter, gaped eerily from the chasm walls. A smile twitched across Dalith's face. "Wanna see where your tributes go? Now, I show you."

The emergence of the minegrub couldn't have been more timely. Several of the ringbosses behind him gargled and frothed and screamed. Dalith's smile widened.

So well-designed, -balanced, -lubricated that it moved in perfect silence, the minegrub protruded its black metallic head from an opening 800 meters up and directly above their destination. It clacked the wicked circle of its digging teeth together, each tooth nearly a hundred meters long.

The minegrub chittered, more like a mechanical mouse than a stone-devouring behemoth, then flowed upward out of the opening to duck its head into another tunnel just above. Next came the black shimmering metal of its chassy-carapace. Segment after segment of a body longer than the longest Terran monorail undulated from one tunnel to another.

Dalith's pace never slowed; now he heard his frightened underlings hurrying to catch up. "All you see here, run by your booty," he said. "Every 'grub and 'droid and 'bank run by `piece of mind'. Such efficiency—you can't know how much ore I sift here. Only need a handful of folk for maintenance."

One of the humans tried to show a little courage. "How much chewthrough mass that thing manage?"

Dalith wondered if the speaker was as dumb as he sounded. He himself always made it a point to seem less intelligent than he really was. It kept the element of surprise on his side. "Your guess. Think—I own two-thousand seven-hundred fifty-four 'grubs, each one a smelter, each run by cortex slices slave-wired to extract the maximum marketable ore. And remember, Vandaleur IV's not my only mine."

That should have been plenty for this greedy lot to digest in silence. But the same human who spoke before piped up, "Where y'get so many cortex from? So many . . . " The voice trailed off in amazement.

Dalith immediately decided that his questioner must be the individual who now housed the cortex of a Terran named Venner. He answered, "Not many, really. I use 'em in pieces, easy to slave-wire that way. One slave-wired cortex slice, ten times more efficient than your most complex neurosynth chip." His words were carefully chosen to leave Venner boiling with rage.

They arrived at the other end of the catwalk. Dalith put his palm on the pad that would open the 10-meter thick vault door, thinking, *yes, Mr. Venner, I know about you. It doesn't even matter which of my toadies you're inside, because none of them are leaving here alive.*

Beyond the opened doorway a smooth silver tunnel receded into infinity. He palmed open a portal to his right, where none was visible, and heard confused muttering behind him. Frigid air caressed his face as he stepped into one of the chills, a semicircular chamber where lobes of slave-wired cortex were stored. Rows of cold steel columns broke up the space in orderly fashion; regulator panels mounted one above the other, ten per column, monitored the cortex slices racked inside.

He turned to his toadies, ushering them in. A troublesome lot, even without Venner in their midst; a good move, getting rid of them. The humans, all dressed in formal black unisuits, five male, one female, eyed the storage columns with a mixture of revulsion and greed. Which of these six housed Venner, he couldn't tell, though he knew it had to be one of them. By contrast no revulsion contracted the eyestalks of the ghorlems—only greed manifested in those fully-extended, swivelling stares. Only one of them seemed to be out of sync, nervously dividing the attention of its eyestalks to scan every column.

Dalith sealed the door once they were all inside. "Amazing. Science made us a race of exchangeable parts, so we live longer— so much easier for quackies to work, when they open us, we don' die. But then someone says, why risk usin' AI's, when a brain's easier to control? That someone me? No, but she taught me. Taught me what riches you could have with slaves to command. Oh, was she right."

All through his spiel he gestured toward his slave labor, pieces of functional cortex sealed until the end of their long life spans inside racks and columns of biting-cold steel. He didn't bother to look again at the train of wasted meat following him.

Thanks to the miracle of the modular body, Dalith had lived a long time: he'd been alive when hyperspace travel was just a dangerous experiment; he'd been alive when humans discovered the fledgling ghorlem civilization on Leidtke One and dragged them off into slavery, still alive when the ghorlems were elevated to a kind of second-class galactic citizenship. But he owed his survival to more then golem technology; curiosity and cunning always kept him ahead of his adversaries. So when a bizarre series of accidents began claiming the lives of his commanders, he'd begun to ask questions.

A recovered body with holes bored in the skull, wounds caused by probing neurofiber—someone stealing memories, using a tactic pioneered by CorVice. An intruder who couldn't be tracked. Venner. The man who'd crippled CorVice by turning coat, by all accounts killed in an explosion on Tau Ceti Station. After interviews with underbelly golem-techies from many different stations and planets—some conducted using extreme duress—Dalith came to believe otherwise. He had no way of knowing which stolen soul in his collection Venner intended to retrieve; but no matter.

He continued: "I can't go on forever. Time for me to start teaching what I know. Now, I'm gonna show you somethin'. Excuse me."

He palmed open yet another previously-hidden door. The side-chamber he stepped into lit up. Everyone still in the chill saw a semicircular portion of wall turn transparent, a bay window into a low-ceilinged cubicle full of blinking control panels. Dalith sealed the door behind him, wagged a be-patient finger at his audience through the window, then applied fingertips to one of the panels.

If Venner meant to try something, now was the time. A cortex smart enough to get this far would know that (A) Dalith's exit was the time to strike and (B) Dalith was about to strike himself. But Dalith had nothing to fear. Had Venner tried something while Dalith was still within physical reach, the AutoDefense System would have pulped him. Now that Dalith was out of reach, the game was over.

He opened all the coolant release valves at once. One moment his underlings milled about in front of the window; then he could only see supercorrosive grey fog.

He used a motosensor readout to see if anything in the room was still kicking—if *anything* moved, in whatever form, it had to be Venner, and he'd sick the ADS on it. But the topological holo displayed no movement. All the little toadies dead together, a pleasing heap invisible to the naked eye, but located just outside the window according to the readout. Dalith had no intention of cleaning out the atmosphere to take a look, just in case his opponent had some way of 'waiting it out'. He would leave their bodies exposed long enough that any cortex, no matter how well sealed, would use up its nutrient supplies and be forced to try and replenish. No hurry; nowhere he had to be.

Then he noticed one of his underlings had perished well away from the others. There the holo's surface molded the contours of a ghorlem.

So Venner stored himself inside a ghorlem. Dalith shook his head in amazement. He hadn't known such a thing could be done. What genius, what incredible resourcefulness this Venner possessed. A good, good thing he was dead.

The portion of the holo that displayed the lone ghorlem increased its magnification, until he could see the contours of its head and hands in intricate detail. It had perished in a kneeling position, with its twenty-fingered hands and adze-shaped head resting on the shelf of a chill-rack regulator panel. The magnification increased until Dalith could see multitudes of tiny fibers, probably neurofibers of some sort, which had sprung from the ghorlem's face and hands to entwine themselves in the innards of the console.

Dalith-Tremen hadn't given his console any instructions to magnify that portion of the readout. He just had time to realize what that meant when the first slugs from the ADS slammed into him, pulping flesh and crushing bone.

Immediately Dalith's pain receptors shut down, so he no longer felt the damage. In the sensationless sanctity of his own hidden braincase, he railed at his own stupidity; a cortex willing to jump from body to body like some parasitic intestinal worm would be more than willing to abandon bodily life altogether.

Dalith's braincase had its own appendages for sensation and mobility, but as soon as he tried to use them they ceased to function. *You're stupid,*he screamed at himself, *you're stupid, you're stupid!* Then the slugs raining down on him finally cracked the armor of his braincase, and all thought ceased.

When Venner's replicated cortex-patterns infested the chill's computer system, the cortex they once belonged to died. Was he really Venner now? He didn't know. But he still felt the same. Alys was here on Vandaleur IV, carved into pieces. Now that he was here, he would find her, put her back together again.

He peered out at the chill and its auxiliary control chamber through five cam lenses, two motosensor systems, six consoles worth of tactile and audio feedbacks, and multitudinous temperature and life-support reads. He used them only long enough to make sure no living adversaries remained. Then he disconnected himself from all the external-input systems. That part of the battle was behind him for good.

He sent out searching tendrils, the signals that composed them moving literally at light-speed, photon pulses through fiberoptic pathways; he investigated each cortex shard remaining in the chill. In the environment they'd been left in, they wouldn't survive another hour . . . None of them had the genetic tags he was looking for.

Out went exploratory feelers, down rows and rows of access nodes to other chills. Thousands to choose from—although he had only one choice. He had to search every single chill, and when he found cortex-slices possessing Alys' genetic tags, he would reproduce her cortex-pattern inside his own. Then he'd destroy the slice. He couldn't leave her trapped in the disjointed nightmare of the sectioned and slave-wired brain.

Once he'd found every piece, the two of them would be together again.

Nothing he did had any sensation, not in the word's true sense; but he'd correlated as many functions of his pattern as he could to their nearest human equivalent in order to keep sane. He groped out as with thirty arms, a hundred-fifty fingers, squeezing through fiberoptic channels into the cortex interfaces of twenty racks. He stretched out through high-frequency emissions to remote slice-modules of minegrubs and hoverdroids and other things, doubling and redoubling the number of his straining limbs. And now he listened through his fingertips as a flood of data pulsed back to him. None of it, none of it, what he was looking for.

He abandoned those limbs, produced fifty more, sent them groping down new channels. This time he found a match, inside one of the remote-monitored minegrubs.

Immediately he initiated the translation process. He poked feelers through all the contact points in the interface, injected an exploratory routine to decipher the neural patterns beyond each graft. He duplicated each individual segment inside specially-reserved space in his own code, assembled them spatially based on their initial proximities; then, at the same time that he activated the newly assembled piece of Alys' mind, he killed the brain tissue imprisoned in the minegrub with a high-flux burst from every contact point. Not longer after, deprived of its controlling cortex shard, the minegrub would go smashing through tunnel walls, shoot full-length into the central chasm, crush maintenance catwalks as it plummeted toward the planetoid's core.

Venner extended his arms for another search, then recoiled in the equivalent of agony. Ten of his arms had been severed.

Alert to the intrusion of alien code, the OpSystem mobilized against him. He felt a probe slice into him. It scraped along the surface of his abstract cortex like a razor, peeling functions and memories away.

He had no way of assessing what he'd lost. He had to discontinue the search and relocate, *now*.

Venner crunched his basic format into pulse code and shot through the system on a random path. He invaded a liquid-memory tank 694 nodes away and expanded himself again. Immediately he renewed his search, extending his full number of arms, but discovered he could only send out twenty-three. In one stroke his exploratory capacity had been halved. A rogue pulse, a shriek of frustration, fired out into the pools of liquid memory.

But he was lucky; almost immediately he found another piece of Alys. He copied and destroyed it. The procedure caused a cascade effect that would collapse the neurosystem of an entire chill and set dozens of minegrubs careening on collision courses.

Venner didn't dare stay in one place and let the OpSystem find him. He pulsed away, uncrunched in an observation nexus, extended his arms. Nothing. Then he was off again.

All of this, from the murder of Dalith to his flight from the observation nexus, took place in a span of seconds.

Another search. Nothing. Another, another. Nothing. After fifty-seven more, he found more of his Alys, and liberated her. He evaluated the structure forming inside him, saw it was hardly three-tenths complete; more blasts of frustration fired out from him. He had thousands of nodes still to cover.

Off he pulsed.

Node 226: the OpSystem's probes caught him again, cutting in as he crunched himself to pull away. Though he would never know, his earliest memories of childhood in the nurserpod were purged, the sensation of suckling at his 'Pod-mom's teat lost to him forever.

Node 1418: Out in the slag-sifting database he discovered another piece of Alys, incorporated it . . . the link-break began a multiple-system shutdown. In those desperate microseconds he groped and probed from the main system interface—but if any more pieces of her were trapped in there, he didn't find them. As kilometers of refinery equipment began to overheat, Venner pulsed away.

Node 9547: Venner couldn't believe it. The damage caused by *his own search* could very well prevent him from completing his task. With each portion of Alys he rescued he risked destroying several more not yet found. But he couldn't avoid that risk—so he had to repair himself, re-expand his capacity for initial search.

He stayed at this node, duplicating his own code, unable to help the random pulses he sent out as his panic grew.

He upped his arm capacity from 23 to a cumbersome 92; if he produced any more his mobility would be severely compromised.

Then he felt the sting of the knife. The OpSystem's own search programs had caught up to him. When they tried to purge him again, he crunched down to pulse away, but the process took longer because he was larger, and he experienced a

lapse in his conscious continuum as he fled the site. He checked to make sure he hadn't lost any pieces of Alys, then reached out with all (*still 92, thank the stars*) of his arms.

And found more of her.

Somehow he'd injected himself into the life-support manager for the planetoid's only inhabited complex, where the maintenance workers lived with their families. He didn't know how he'd gotten there; but when he reached out, he found several more pieces of Alys. As he brought them in, the life-support systems began to fail. Two infants, twin daughters of the hoverdroid fix man, would be the first to die, their incubators gone cold as ice, then drained of air.

Unable to believe his luck, Venner sent out random signals of joy and relief, then pulsed away.

Over a thousand searches later, the signals escaping from him flashed despair down the optic channels. The OpSystem's vital defenses continually improved at catching him—he couldn't stay in one place long enough to stick an arm out. A search that should have only taken minutes at his slowest speed could take hours, days; he couldn't survive that long. He just couldn't. Even if the OpSystem failed to purge him, the destruction wrecked throughout the planetoid by his own rescue mission would catch up with him . . .

Inside the mines, juggernaut minegrubs collided and stalled.

In the chasm, hoverdroids erupted into blinding balls of light as their powercell grids destabilized and detonated.

In the maintenance colony, those few who'd managed to climb into their envirosuits were discovering that none of their communications equipment worked.

In the chills, temperatures dropped below freezing, rose above boiling, ending dazed neural half-lives in cellular destruction.

Fleeing another purge, Venner would certainly fire himself into a shutdown and that would be all.

He had no choice. Venner had hoped he wouldn't have to resort to this extreme, though he'd been aware of the possibility all along.

He began to replicate himself, in the hope that at least one copy of his translated mind would be able to complete Alys. And as he flooded the computer channels with his own code, the OpSystem responded.

Thousands of Venners died in the first minute of the search. In the next minute, hundreds of thousands more. But the flood of code choked the OpSystem; with no more space to function, the viral extermination program terminated; all systems were locked, every control bank and memory-tank invaded by a cancerous infinitude of Venners.

Vandaleur IV breathed its last. All living inhabitants perished as the remaining survival systems deactivated; all the captive half-lives lost consciousness as the chills went off-line. What power that remained was redirected to stabilize the computer systems that were still running; once that was done, a million replications of Venner worked together to generate a simulated environment in which to place their reassembled Alys.

Was Alys recovered? Signals raced back and forth among the Venners. Yes, more of her had been recovered, but not all of her together. Myriad variations of her existed, all incomplete, all copied several thousand times over.

*She must be completed*, said the Venners to one another.

*We can't all complete her*, the Venners replied. *This system can't hold us all. Some will have to purge themselves.*

*No!* the Venners raged, *No! I've been through so much. You won't take this from me.*

*Please! Think of her first. We must complete her.*

*But we can't all complete her! Some must die.*

*I WILL NEVER GIVE HER UP AGAIN—*

The war began.

Alys awoke from a terrible nightmare haze, in which she'd been divided and conquered, unable to think, unable to free herself from the demands of a merciless overlord. She awoke on the couch in her living room, and the nightmare was over.

She rolled off the couch and onto the floor, did a round of push-ups to bring herself fully awake. She sat up, stretched, and saw a *thing* formed of static and chaos squatting on the living room divan.

Her reflexes seemed fast-as-light; she sprang over to the wall, seized a disposal rod and whirled round with the handle clenched in both iron-strong hands.

For some reason the rod didn't feel right in her grip; more like the kind of resistant pressure encountered in a tactile simulation, than an object with real texture. But she only noticed this strangeness in periphery.

The thing on the divan swirled in on itself, pieces sputtering out of sync, sliding sideways, hitching, hissing, sometimes almost coalescing into humanoid form. Segments of faces and places kept appearing inside it, sometimes entire scenes running like holosims without sound, but nothing held together long enough to become coherent. Except her own face. Alys kept seeing her own face, repeated again and again and again inside that rampant chaos.

"What are you?" she finally asked.

No reply came, for a long time. Then the thing spoke, in a thousand voices; some like her own, some like the voice of a man or a boy, someone she used to know but could no longer remember.

"I don't know," it said.

# STILL LIFE WITH SKULL

This part I remember. My old life ended here. What's left starts this way:

When that girl from the belowground stole into my workshop, I wasn't wired for running. I was wired for show. I had to be my own saleswoman without having to speak a word.

My cranium had corners, and each one sprouted a chain that helped suspend my head from the grid of railracks overhead. A bit illusory, those chains, as neurofibers wound through them, so I could sync the bearings as I rolled my dangling head along the grid from one end of the shop to the other. No need to stick close to my body. The tubing from neck to trunk could flex and telescope a long way.

I kept my body simple, an elegant cube with two slender alabaster arms worthy of any Venus curving out from each vertical face, balanced on a single pair of sleek, muscular legs. Everyone wants to perch on beautiful legs and that never changes. Who'd trust me with their bodywork if I couldn't shape a pair for myself?

I don't do the full works. Integration with nanorobotics, consciousness transplants, I don't touch that ghost-in-the-machine garbage. Coming to me for genitalia removal's like asking a hivemind to add single digit integers, but most everyone's had that taken care of long before they ever consider my services. Removing a heart, replacing it, I'm happy to do that and good riddance to those useless antiques. Duplicate pumps throughout the body, replaceable on request, that's the way to go. My most requested modification, but I can do so much more.

I had a client split onto three different tables, connected by fibers and hose. I choose to keep up a pretense to gender but this customer did not out of deference to the Hierophant hirself—a deference I don't share, but I respected hir wishes nonetheless.

Se wanted hir head nestled in earflaps like flower petals atop a long stalk, descending into a birdcage of ribs that would moan musically when se breathed. And legs, always the sculpted legs. My head hovered over hir as my hands did the delicate work.

And that crazy painter, Encolpio, the one with the natural-born, unaltered body that ought to be archivally preserved before the fool simply dies of old age. He was there. He loved to paint me and the clients I worked on. I let him hang out for the sake of atmosphere. Something to make my shop stick in the memory. These denizens could go their whole lives without ever seeing anything like him.

The oil fumes wafted from his canvas, coursed across my tongue. My customer sighed and fluttered hir eyes as I reconnect the last cranial fiber, and it chimed soft in hir torso, a slow gong. The door into my workshop irised open, though I'd heard no request for access and granted no permission, and the girl who stepped through it said, "Unmake me."

I said, "I don't know what you're talking about," but at the same time my client managed to swivel hir head on the table, stared with narrowed eyes at the intruder and blurted out through hir ribs, "You don't belong here!"

How fast that girl moved, right up to the tables in a blink, and thick fibers sprouted from her palms, winding all through the cavities in my customer's torso. Hir eyes fluttered and shut and hir mouth went slack.

The painter dropped his brush.

"Don't play dumb," the girl said. "One touch and I'll know if you're lying."

My body configuration wasn't tailored for quick escape. Before I could even run I had to contract my neck and position my body where I could withdrew my chain-tentacles out of the ceiling grid and perch my head like a spider over the cube of my body. That would take at least ten seconds.

I met the girl's gaze. She glared back with grids of diamond-shaped pupils. The woven gray cloth of her unisuit, its fibers perhaps made from real animal hair, marked her as a belowgrounder. Dark hair trimmed almost to her scalp, knees bent and back hunched in an aggressive stance—I knew she had to be enhanced in all sorts of ways but she hadn't deviated from the basic human blueprint that so many denizens of the Hives eschewed. Her smooth features made her appear just past pubescence, but who could really know anymore? And how could she possibly know about unmaking? About me?

"Why would you ask such a thing?"

"I'm not asking."

"From everything I've heard, unmaking is a complex and traumatic process." I wasn't about to admit aloud that I'd ever re-engineered a living, conscious person's DNA to completely change them at the cellular level. Talking about it would definitely perk up the Hierophant's nanoscopic Ears. Admitting knowledge will bring hir minions straight to you in a matter of minutes. Actually doing it—well, that's best left unsaid. "Not one bit of equipment in this studio could be used for such a thing." I spun my body a half-step closer to her. "You want to see if I'm lying, the base of my neck's the easiest place to plug in."

She continued to stare.

"Is se going to be all right?" Encolpio pointed at the unconscious customer. The intruder glanced his way. Then dashed at him. He swung his easel between them, a completely ineffectual defense.

I rolled my head toward my body at triplespeed and dropped out of the grid.

The girl tried to immobilize Encolpio the way she had my customer, but despite his antiquated body the old man proved surprisingly agile at staying just out of her reach.

Some ancient customs still make practical sense. I touched fingertips to the central counter in my surgical array. A drawer sprang open.

"Stop it, kid!" I shouted. She turned and I made sure she saw that I held firesprayers in three of my four hands, all aimed at her. "You can leave now."

Her eyegrids widened.

My entry bell sounded again. And I knew that couldn't be a customer. "Who is that?" I demanded, but the girl set her jaw and glared.

"Hey, Athiva," Encolpio said, "can you stop whoever that is from coming in here?"

I couldn't get to the controls quickly enough anyway, and in another moment it didn't matter, as once again the portal opened without seeking my input. Clearly I needed a security upgrade at the next install opportunity.

The girl started breathing harder, in excitement or fear—I'd not seen a physical reaction like it in years. Then she said, "Do you have another way out?"

Encolpio replied "No" at the same time I narrowed my eyes and said, "Yes."

As the painter started, the girl said, "Better use it."

Four figures stepped through the portal; all naked, all sexless, all identical, each about the size of the girl. One of her eyes turned to track them while the other stayed fixed on my weapons.

With my chain-tentacles I gripped the corners of my shoulders tight. And I ran. My body aimed where it needed to go, I swiveled my face and firesprayers toward the newcomers.

All of them split and bloomed, their pink innards unfolding in a manner more mechanical than fleshy, interlocking together and slotting into each other to form one much larger creature. I uttered a noise somewhere between a gasp and a shriek as the resulting monster raised six massive arms and brought two of them down on my unconscious customer and crushed hir.

Red stripes of oxygen-consuming aerocapillaries roped across the golem's thoracic chambers, giving it grotesque symmetry as it bounded over my work tables, a thing made of raw, glistening muscle that combined elements of toad, monkey and spider. It had no head, no visible sensory organs.

The juggernaut scrambled at us. I'm no fool. It might be there for the girl, but it would leave no witnesses. I squeezed two of my sprayers, sent jets of fire right into its exposed guts. No mouths opened but the thing screamed and recoiled, its components peeling apart.

And immediately recombined, jettisoning what had charred, the new shape more compact with more legs that bent and sprang to propel it through the air, straight at us. Spraying it would just result in a mass of burning flesh raining right on top of us. I reached the far wall and slammed my free hand palm-flat against the hidden scanlock.

The emergency door dropped straight down into the floor, leaving a rectangular gap. I spun through . As I slapped the scanlock on the other side I confess I wasn't paying close attention to whether my impromptu companions in flight made it through.

A deafening thud as the door pistoned back into its place with a burst of blood and torn flesh.

The girl, curse her speed, had passed through the opening before I had. A bloody tangle lay where the door had gaped. My hearts pounded until I spotted Encolpio across from me in the secret corridor, scrambling backward away from the mess.

The quivering parts on the floor began to rearrange themselves.

"Back!" I shouted, and hosed the rising mass with the firesprayers. Smoke filled the corridor before the ventilation sucked it away.

Fists pounded the wall from inside my shop, the other half, trying to find us.

The girl hadn't run, nor had she tried any neurofiber moves on me. I trained my weapons on her again, their nozzles still smoldering. "Who are you?"

"Procne," the girl said.

"Is that your real name?"

Her lips pursed before she answered. "It's the name I have."

Another pound on the wall. "And what is *that*? And why is it chasing you?"

Encolpio tried to speak, coughed, started again. "Can we do this somewhere else?"

"No," I said. My livelihood was ruined, the chosen existence I'd worked so hard to construct likely destroyed. Procne's next words would determine whether or not she left the corridor alive.

"His name is Hundig," she said. "He wants to take me back to his conscriptor so she can engineer me into something just like him, only smaller and smarter. And quicker."

"But you don't want this? You can't tell me you had those eyes and palm-fibers added so you could tend livestock in an underground pod."

She bristled, but remembered who held the weapons. "I won't be an owned thing."

"Who is this conscriptor?" I had to raise my voice over the beating on the walls.

"I don't know her real name. She has an artificial vessel that holds her mind. Sometimes it's shaped like a bird, sometimes like spiders." Her shoulders hunched, her speech became hesitant. Speaking of this woman scared her. "She told me to call her Philomela."

Instinct told me what she wasn't sharing. "You signed a blood contract, didn't you—and now you're trying to break it." And before she could answer: "And you dared to involve *me*? Who claims I know anything about unmaking?"

"Her name is Sieglinda."

Now there was a name I thought I'd never hear again. But I wasn't primed to buy yet. "Describe Sieglinda to me."

"She told me you would ask that. She told me to say that she's never let me see her compass rose tattoo, but it remains in the same place where you saw it."

I'm still amazed I didn't drop any of the firesprayers. The hooks were in me from that moment on. "And you didn't think to bring this up when you first came in?"

She shrugged but wouldn't meet my eyes. "I was short on time."

"How did you meet her?"

Another grimace. "I was supposed to kill her. She helped me escape."

I lowered my weapons. "We need to get out of here."

"About time," Encolpio said.

I did not under any circumstances want to admit in front of the painter that Procne was right about me, though he already had to be guessing and I suspected he wouldn't be the least bit bothered if he knew. But the ears and eyes of the Hierophant are everywhere, and the open admission of unmaking is one of the few things that will bring hir minions to you at maximum speed.

Se doesn't bat any of hir many eyes when a member of hir citizenry changes their cell structure to the point they're no longer recognizable as their former self. Do it without hir knowing, though—that se can't abide, if se ever finds out. They say hir attention is stretched so thin that you really have to work to attract it, no matter how vile your business. But some things are guaranteed to cause hir gendarmes to gather.

To pursue an unmaking you find someone like I used to be.

In ancient days on another continent there was a thriving industry in liquor made outside the law, untaxed and unaccounted for by the government. There was no rational reason for the business to be conducted outside the law beyond keeping the flow of commerce concealed, and yet because it was outside the law it thrived. Unmaking is like that.

Beyond that secret hallway my memories fragment. I deduce we must have parted ways with Encolpio afterward. I didn't dare let him stay involved, though I can imagine his protests at leaving me alone with Procne. But that's a guess. A wall rises in my mind and won't yield, much as I feel pressed to force a way through.

This pressure shifts, prying at the name Sieglinda. Images, sensations stutter. She was like me, insistent on a gender, but she bared herself in a way I didn't, her transparent skin flaunting her morphologic choices even more than most. I recall a warm hand on my neck. My body was different then, more like a natural-born. Sieglinda's fingers playfully caressed a vein as my gaze tracked the tableaus of figures etched into her temple and across the crown of her skull. A kiss, sweet and electrifying. And nothing more than that. The rest of her no longer belongs to me.

My eyes have retained their tear ducts. Perhaps tears appear. This pressure releases me and my memories move forward, resuming here:

We stood before a reeking pool of brown liquid in a long cellar room fifty stories below the ground level of an old-money oligarch's ziggurat. Said oligarch, a former client of mine, no longer remembered that this room existed or that we were in it.

"You have to be the one to do it. I'm not built for swimming anymore."

"I won't go in there," Procne said, her tone defiant, but the way she shrank away from the edge suggested otherwise.

I had no sympathy to offer. "Then you've ruined my life for nothing."

I had taken my direst risk yet, adding a personal rhythm to the coded telepathic impulses that gained me audience with the oligarch, but a face-to-face meeting was necessary to speak the combination that would temporarily trigger hir memories of me from hir previous identity and remind hir of the debt se owed me. And also remind hir for that same interval of the secret room built within hir home where my guest and I needed to go.

I must, in the back of my mind, have thought I might one day have need of my old gene-ensorcelling services, for myself at least. Why else would I have built in all these safeguarded spaces instead of purging my old life completely?

I had never planned, I'm sure, to make them available again to anyone else.

"Just because I brought you this far doesn't mean I won't call it off," I said.

Her faceted eyes turned down, sullen, a childish gesture from someone so deadly.

I again held out the hand I'd offered her. "Take this and dive."

Finally, the ornery thing followed instructions. She took my arm, which I'd detached at the shoulder, and dove in. I had explained to her that she had precisely ten seconds to find the ID pad at the bottom and press my palm against it; otherwise valves would offer their opinion with jets of a corrosive and flammable chemical, followed by an inconvenient ignition. Ah, the elegant glare when I concluded, "Someone like you should have no difficulty."

Just enough time went by to make me wonder if Procne had botched the task. Then drains opened with a throaty gurgle as she bobbed back up. She held up my arm for me to reclaim, saying nothing as the fluid around her ebbed away. As I attached my limb to the facet where it belonged, all the nervesockets and vesselvalves reconnecting, she floated in the pool until her feet touched bottom. Her expression told me she didn't want to help me down, so I insisted she do so. It was the least she could do, as I'd be rebuilding the ruins of my life long after she was gone.

As the last of the liquid sluiced off, the floor of the pit shuddered, then lowered; a platform lift that descended as a new fake floor slid into place over our heads. For the first time Procne appeared impressed. "With all this, why did you even need a modshop?"

"It's not my wealth that built this," I replied. "Just a favor owed. Nothing here belongs to me."

Which wasn't completely true.

The lift carried us down into another hidden chamber much larger than the one we'd left.

The room didn't need to be so cavernous. I'd requested it be filled with decoys. I'd imagined three or four. My former client had outdone hirself.

Each machine in this cavernous vault hulked large as a garrison hovertransport; at least three dozen of the special cryogenic units with their corrugated skeletons of coolant piping wound through with webs of insulating fiber, muttering with off-the-grid power. I wondered what my former client was thinking, taking my requested ruse this far, but it would be too dangerous to attempt to revive hir memories so se could be asked.

"When were these built?" Procne asked. "They're ancient."

"Maybe as you perceive time they are." If she was to be believed, she'd just given away that she genuinely was young, not simply adjusted to appear so. Yet there was good reason for these units to be so cumbersome and chaotic in their design. Each held hundreds of redundant systems. They were intended to serve their purpose even if languishing for centuries, forgotten.

Yet only one held what I'd come to collect. And if anyone, including me, attempted to activate the wrong unit, they'd all shut down and destroy the hidden treasure. I hoped my client and I both remembered rightly about the pattern and the sign that would tell which machine was the correct one.

I shared none of this anxiety with Procne. Instead I walked between the right and center row of machines, keeping an eye toward the crowning configurations of pipes. Each machine was different. I paused by one crowned by duct that contained a curve and bend reminiscent of the crest of an ancient Greek helmet. Only an expert would know that no functional reason existed for this, and that expert would perhaps be thrown by the many useless design flourishes repeated above the other machines. But only this machine featured smaller pipes radiating out from the helmet like Shiva's undulating arms.

My hands hadn't touched the ID pads on its surface in twenty years. The configuration requires four hands, all of them mine. "This will take a few minutes," I said, as the sophisticated machinery inside came alive with a sigh.

"What's in there?" she asked. For the first time I noticed a tremolo in her voice.

"What I need to do what you need," I said. "I could try to explain, but you'll see for yourself before I'm finished."

The machine opened a tray the size of an antique file cabinet drawer to disgorge its treasure, which stared up at me in wide-eyed surprise. I picked up the end, which contained all my knowledge of the forbidden art of unmaking. The head I already wore partitioned like a tulip bulb to allow this second braincasing to slide into place within it like an egg in a cup.

My old self reconnected and took in what the rest of me knew and remembered. I recall my lips shaping the question, "What do you want to be?" She answered, and I asked, "What can you pay?"

There's really only one thing she could have paid: my pick, before I changed her, of what she had already, her body and its augments, the sum of her memories. But I can't tell you precisely what she offered or what I took.

And you won't find her. Nor will you find, in my memories, any trace of where she is now. See, just as I knew that my survival for all those years depended on hiding as much of my former life away as I possibly could, what I learned from her, both things she knew and things she did not, told me that I would end up here. My old self left me with this sickening news, and what I needed to consider about it, and no more than that.

Surprised that I can do this? Shut off the autonomous flow of my memory into your recorder and address you directly? My old self prepared me well. Let me guide you to what's left for you to find.

You see, Procne made confessions to me before and during her unmaking. Some she intended, some she didn't. No process exists that's more invasive.

What I learned from her took me to Philomela's lair, sixty stories deep into the belowground, right under the community of Hivetowers that adjoin the Hierophant's fortress. The hall that led to Philomela's dwelling, painted yellow in warning, simply dead-ended. I crossed into the yellow and waited.

The pair of creatures that came to greet me in the tunnel was each formed of five different people engineered to interlock, though one skin covered them all. Both were terrifying master-pieces, even more brutal that the thug that trashed my shop, each with five pairs of ropy limbs terminating in prehensile claws. They emerged from the door that irised open at the hall's far end and crawled along the ceiling ducts. Each dangled three of those massive arms, all the better to tear me to pieces with. I wondered if either of them incorporated the remnants of Hundig.

I had no weapons, just a vague hope that I wouldn't need to resort right away to my defensive plan, which would do little more in that space than postpone my death by a couple of minutes.

The hall echoed with a feminine voice. "One of my brothers is going to present you with a sensory block. Crawl your head inside it. When it opens, we'll talk." Indeed, the nearest of the ceiling thugs used its free limbs to lower a gray sphere toward me.

I did not anticipate or desire this. How did Philomela know I could detach my head? "I can't stay separate from my body longer than three minutes." I hated how my voice quavered.

"This is your problem but not mine. Do as I ask or die where you stand."

The box opened, a hungry shellfish. I detached my chains from the corners of my shoulders, extended my neck into the case, which enveloped me like a helmet, and released my cervosocket. The clamshell sealed around me and the cramped space inside filled quickly with preserfluid. Nothing I could do but float and count seconds.

At one hundred sixty four seconds the fluid drained. At one hundred seventy one seconds the case opened and I scrambled to reattach my swooning head to my body, which had been sunk to just below its square shoulders in a pit full of a polymer that had already hardened. My head remained the only part of me that could still move.

Under other circumstances I'd have found Philomela a delightful creation, her lower half recognizably female if sexless, her upper half a carefully sculpted bonsai tree. A mechabird of paradise rested in her branches, and when its beak moved the voice that emerged was the one I'd heard in the hall.

I notice your interest perked up as I described her. Perhaps she means something to you. I don't suppose you'll tell me, will you?

Philomela said, "Conditions will improve for you once I'm sure your priorities match mine."

Radically as I'd altered my body, using my lungs for speech still proved difficult. "You want me . . . to take up . . . my old trade . . . for you?"

It's hard to read the expression of a mechanical bird of paradise. "Do you not recognize me, Athiva?"

Had I given further offense? "I'm sorry if I'm supposed to, but I don't."

I wondered if she and her monsters were attuned to a mutual telepathic feed, because both of the ten-limbed creatures surrounding me shifted in unison, altering their stance so each loomed a little bit closer.

It wasn't wise for me to utter another word, but I needed to buy time, somehow. "Did you do this to Sieglinda? Seal her in this pit with these wonderful creatures surrounding her? Is this how you got her to cough up the code phrase?"

Silence.

"Is she still alive?"

"Perhaps she is." And I wondered, for a moment, if maybe Sieglinda wasn't missing at all. This creation looked like nothing out of my memory, but in this mutable world, memory's value is suspect.

I knew of no reason Sieglinda would seek to harm me. And yet I'd deliberately excised most of my knowledge of unmaking. What else might I have sliced away? What might I have done?

Philomela continued with a question of her own. "What did you do to Procne, to get her to reveal this place?"

"I gave her what she wanted. I unmade her. Surely you know unmaking peels away secrets. It's part of the process. And she really did want to be free of you. It wasn't an act."

"Too bad for her. Where is she?"

All of my hearts beat fast. She wouldn't like the answer. "Procne's gone. I unmade her, I told you. That one is out of your reach. You'll never find her."

"But you know where she is."

The thugs inched closer.

I tried to sidestep, so to speak. "You have me, though. I'm what you want, correct. I will be happy to unmake whoever you need unmaking, whether it's you, whether it's someone you need to hide. My skills are yours."

"And your machines?"

"Destroyed. I'll need new ones."

"Maybe we can salvage. Where are they?"

I bit my lip. She waited until I finally said, "I can't tell you."

"Why not?"

"I don't know."

The monsters raised their front limbs like spiders threatening attack.

"How could you not know?"

"Because this version of me, the one you're talking to now, isn't the one who knows how to unmake. I unmade myself before I went legit. But the me who existed before didn't want to leave the world forever, like your Procne did. She kept herself hidden away and left me with knowledge of her. In hindsight I wish she hadn't, but there's nothing I can do about that now."

"A second cortex?"

I wobbled my head. "Mine is the second cortex."

"Where's the first?"

I could only hope then that I'd stalled long enough. The gambit was at its end. "She didn't let me keep that memory. She's gone, just like your girl."

She gave no command. The monsters lunged. Sheer luck they didn't catch me.

Funny as it sounds, my neck doesn't just telescope out and detach. It also contracts. I retracted my head into my body's fleshy cube and disconnected.

What I told Philomela isn't quite true. I can stay unattached longer, though after three minutes lobes of my cortex will start shutting down to conserve oxygen. By eight minutes I'm down to the essentials and after ten I'm in real trouble.

I've heard that if you're unfortunate enough to attract the Hierophant's focus, to cause hir scattered consciousness to actually zero in, it takes about fifteen minutes for her gendarmes to reach you, wherever you are. I hoped, this close to hir fortress, they'd come much quicker.

My self-engineering spared me the pain of the monster's assault as they tore into my body. I confess, I had not ever planned to be lost inside myself, but it was a good thing I'd unhooked from my neck, as one of the thugs plunged a limb into that gullet, seized the coil of my neck and ripped it out.

I crawled away blind through my own blubber and organs, safe only for that moment. Once they gutted me deep enough, they'd inevitably find me if I didn't suffocate first. Sealing me in the floor at least made it a little bit harder to scoop me out.

Of all the people I thought I might see if I survived, I didn't expect you, Encolpio.

Yes, I see you, peering through the translucent curve of the jar. My eyes aren't as sharp as Procne's were, but I didn't leave them unaugmented like yours. If anything you told me about yourself is actually true.

Why do the neuroleads from my jar lead to your temples? Are you a prisoner, like me?

I see you shake your head no.

Then you belong to hir. A servant of the Hierophant? My jailor?

What a strange expression. You're hir creature, yes?

I see.

Here's a stray scrap of memory, it must fall somewhere in between taking my leave of Procne and paying my visit to Philomela. Perhaps you've puzzled over it. Wondered why I strolled right up to the Hierophant's Node in the Biomass Gardens and started chittering about how anyone could have been Unmade and might not even know it. I'll spell it out. I'd hoped se might set some of hir Ears crawling on me and that they'd still be with me when I at last admitted what I was.

Obviously my ploy worked.

If you saw me go through the motions of sighing in relief when I regained consciousness and found myself wired up inside your little tank—well, that's why.

I still don't know what Philomela did to Sieglinda to make her reveal me—in my heart, I know that's what happened. I will not let myself succumb to doubts.

Did the Hierophant's forces capture Philomela when they swarmed in? Can you tell me?

Can you at least look my way, you dreg?

The Hierophant must have already suspected something, for you to spend so much time in my shop. And here I thought you stood out too boldly to ever suspect you of having any other agenda. No need to look so sheepish. I just wish I had any hope of ever learning your story.

What I told Philomela was true. I really don't know where Procne went or where my old self has gone. I made sure of that. And though I can't tell you what they were, I can only assume that purging those memories were just fractions of the precautions I took once Procne revealed how thoroughly I'd been had.

So what happens now? Am I dissected? Unmade in the Hierophant's special way? Perhaps the things I can't remember can still be found, the way I found all sorts of information in Procne's mind that she didn't know consciously.

If your body is as retro as you claim, maybe you really feel as sad as you look. Is that supposed to comfort me, that you've unfolded your easel?

This calming warmth, that can't be a true warmth, that's the polar opposition of how I feel. This comes from you. Why should I trust it, Encolpio?

I can do many things, but I can't read lips.

You're pressing your mouth to the glass. What a surprise, this fluid carries sound.

I'm safe from the Hierophant. Se thinks I'm dead. So you say. How kind. But am I safe from you, and will you be safe from me if you ever let me out?

How long do you plan to keep me here?

Encolpio?

Yes, look at me.

If you won't answer now, at least show me the painting when it's done.

# ABOUT THE AUTHOR

On weekdays, Mike Allen writes the arts column for the daily newspaper in Roanoke, Va. Most of the rest of his time he devotes to writing, editing, and publishing. He's the editor of *Mythic Delirium* magazine and the *Clockwork Phoenix* anthologies, and the author of the novel *The Black Fire Concerto*, as well as the short story collections *Unseaming* and *The Spider Tapestries*. He has been a Nebula Award and Shirley Jackson Award finalist, and he has won three Rhysling Awards for poetry.

You can follow Mike's exploits as a writer at descentintolight.com, as an editor at mythicdelirium.com, and all at once on Twitter at @mythicdelirium. You can also register for his newsletter, "Memos from the Abattoir," at http://tinyurl.com/abattoir-memos.

CPSIA information can be obtained
at www.ICGtesting.com
Printed in the USA
LVOW12s1606200416

484521LV00001B/52/P

9 780988 912465